PRAISE FOR *LEAP*

'This novel is my kind of story; what matters is not described or explained to us, and so we trust and find tender resolve. Myfanwy's uncomplicated prose conveys journeys that are everything but uncomplicated. Engaging and luminous story-telling.' –Rosalie Ham, author of *The Dressmaker*

'An engrossing and compassionate novel that beautifully illuminates the complex interplay of grief, laughter, passion and joy.' –Paddy O'Reilly, author of *The Wonders*

'As I read *Leap*, I often found myself thinking about the characters during the day—each of them crept under my skin and stayed there, their grief and joy becoming part of me. To achieve this is the mark of a fine writer, a writer who knows how to draw us in by portraying what it is to love and lose in a real sense, and also with a sense of mystery.' –Georgia Blain, author of *The Secret Lives of Men*

'A gentle, lyrical, evocative portrait of longing and loss that transforms the fabric of everyday life into luminous vignettes of cinematic detail. This is a tender and surprising book.' –Kalinda Ashton, author of *The Danger Game*

'A taut, sexy novel about heartbreak, redemption and pushing the human body to its limits. Made me feel like an everyday walk down the street could be just one footstep away from flight.' –Fran Cusworth, author of *The Love Child*

'Melbourne comes to life in this engrossing novel, with its varied cast of characters, whip-smart dialogue and intimate sense of place. *Leap* is contemporary, immediate, fast-paced, but also tender and reflective—a rare achievement.' –Lisa Gorton, author of *The Life of Houses*

Myfanwy Jones is the author of *The Rainy Season*, shortlisted for The Melbourne Prize for Literature's Best Writing Award 2009, and co-author of the bestselling *Parlour Games for Modern Families*, Book of the Year for Older Children ABIA 2010. She lives by a creek in Melbourne with her human and non-human family.

LEAP

MYFANWY JONES

ALLEN&UNWIN
SYDNEY·MELBOURNE·AUCKLAND·LONDON

First published in 2015

Allen & Unwin
83 Alexander Street
Crows Nest NSW 2065
Australia
Phone: (61 2) 8425 0100
Email: info@allenandunwin.com
Web: www.allenandunwin.com

Cataloguing-in-Publication details are available
from the National Library of Australia
www.trove.nla.gov.au

ISBN 978 1 92526 611 5

Internal design by Christabella Designs
Set in 12/18.2 Minion Pro by Bookhouse, Sydney
Printed and bound in Australia by McPhersons Printing Group

10 9 8 7 6 5 4 3

MIX
Paper from
responsible sources
FSC
www.fsc.org   FSC® C001695

The paper in this book is FSC® certified.
FSC® promotes environmentally responsible,
socially beneficial and economically viable
management of the world's forests.

For James

Love can do all but raise the Dead
I doubt if even that
From such a giant were withheld
Were flesh equivalent

But love is tired and must sleep,
And hungry and must graze
And so abets the shining Fleet
Till it is out of gaze.

EMILY DICKINSON

L'art du deplacement could be summarised in three words:
running—climbing—jumping.

PARKOURPEDIA

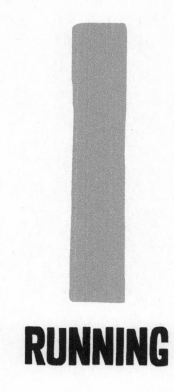

RUNNING

1

She comes when the others are out, announced by Sanjay's
Bollywood door chime; tinny and overwrought, its siren song
ricochets along the ceiling and through his muscles as Joe
takes the five long strides of the corridor. He was looking at
YouTube clips and as he moves towards the door his fists clench
and unclench, fingers unfurl, furl, in a subliminal sequence.

Last days of autumn and the air is like blood: it is hard
to sense where the body ends and the atmosphere begins. He
was not expecting anyone but here she is.

'I saw the sign . . . for the room?' Tipping her head towards
the laundromat next door, the girl is framed by the backlit
doorway. Hands tucked into back pockets, one blue boot

poised behind her on the bottom step, she is at once forward and faltering. Familiar.

He frowns—disoriented. Time opens out, undulates and then compacts. 'Oh . . . right. Yeah.'

She smiles. 'Yeah. Is it still available?'

'The room? It's still empty.' He has remembered the ad Sanjay scribbled on the back of an overdue bill last week, pinned to the community noticeboard beside the soap dispenser; a moment of monetary panic, which has led to this. He tunes in to the turning of the industrial driers, as if their ironclad tempo will settle things. 'So do you want to come in?'

Stands aside to let her past, unprepared for her advent, or how pale and lovely she is. In an antiquated grey tweed jacket, all buttoned-up Katharine Hepburn, she's overdressed and a little breathless, as if she's been running. Her cropped black hair is ruffled and glossy—an animal's pelt rippling to be touched.

He closes the door behind them and the corridor dims; leads the way back down to the kitchen, conscious of the worn carpet patterned with woollen hyacinth and the stale scent of Sanjay's mull bowl. There is no way she is going to want the room.

'Sorry I didn't call first.'

He shrugs. 'Do you want tea or something?' His mother would be pleased.

She rubs her hands together. 'Yeah, sure . . . tea would be good.'

He fills the kettle and rummages for matches in a drawer; releases the gas using a pair of pliers. Turns back, and she is watching him with an intense focus, as if there is something she can't quite decipher or decide.

Drops the pliers onto the counter and smiles. 'This place is a bit decrepit but everything works.' As he says it, he is aware of the holes in his jeans, and his bare feet; of her appraising him, and himself caring.

They sit at the table under the window that looks directly onto the grey paling fence. Jack's ex-girlfriend painted a vine on it with little blood-red flowers that faded to grandma pink. When Jack did the dirty on her she signed off, in tiny lettering along the main artery of the vine, *idiot loser sisterfucker*. It's impossible to see unless you know it is there.

'Have you had much interest? In the room?'

'Yeah, no. We just put up the ad. You're the first.' He clears his throat. 'The room's pretty small. I'll show you.'

They stand again, pushing back chairs, actors in a sloppy play, and walk further up the corridor to the back of the house and into the lean-to. It's more cell than chamber—perfectly white, roughly two metres by three, a bare globe hanging noose-like from the low ceiling. A four-panelled louvre window looks out onto the back garden with its tiny orchard and chook house and rows and rows of cherished greens.

'I like the outlook.'

'Yeah, Sanjay is studying botany. The garden is his.'

'Eighty a week plus bills? That's unheard of, right?'

'Sanjay's dad—Vijay—is the landlord, so until they find him a wife, we're safe. Yeah, so there's the three of us—me, Sanjay and Jack.'

'Hope you're not looking for a mummy.'

'No. Please, no.'

They both smile in the empty white space, right into one another's eyes, and it feels more personal than it should. He stiffens and softens at once, like he is in position on a ledge, counting his breath, ready to jump.

The background clanging of the driers calls them back; he remembers the tea.

In the kitchen, he puts out milk and a bag of sugar and places the steaming cup on the table in front of her, then stands back against the bench, beside the fridge, arms crossed.

Matter of fact: 'We split the bills. There's no landline but reception is okay. We have broadband . . . obviously no washing machine. Sanjay is vegetarian and has his own frying pan.'

She grins, delicate white hands wrapped around the cup. 'Don't touch Sanjay's frying pan.'

'To be honest, we don't eat together much. Sanjay makes curries with stuff from the garden. Jack brings food from his mum's. I eat at work. The fish and chips up the street are good.'

She gets up and walks to the fridge. 'Can I peek? Do you mind?'

'Go ahead.' She is close now, right next to him: bending into the miserable yellow light of the fridge, summing up its miserable contents. He thinks he can smell her—something like trees and water. She is within his reach.

She closes the fridge door and steps back to face him, crossing her arms in his mirror image. He doesn't know if she is mocking him. Yeah, she is.

'I'm a nurse and I only work nights—you'll never see me. I used to live around here but I've been away the past few years. And I'm saving to go again, so I'm definitely interested but I'd probably only be here for a few months. I don't know, could that work for you, maybe?'

He gazes at her from behind his folded arms, noticing the smudges of fatigue under her green eyes, and how they only make her more tangible. 'Yeah, that could work.' He is nodding, head tilted to one side, liking the need in her face. 'The room's yours if you want it.'

'Do you want to, like, consult your housemates?'

'Nah. They'll be happy. Every cent.'

He walks her back up the corridor and it is as if the air in the house has thinned, is colder and lighter. He can feel it now on his skin; it fills him with a melancholic longing. And suddenly he would like to withdraw the offer. He would like the unfathomable girl to walk out the door, down the three steps, and never come back.

'When can I move in?'

So much for pretty manners—she didn't drink the tea. He pours it down the sink, washes and dries the cup and puts it back in the cupboard, all trace of her removed.

In the living room he picks up Jack's guitar and makes some discordant sounds then puts it down again. Only in his imagination will he ever make music. The house looks like shit in her wake, so for a while he straightens up, carrying textbooks and socks and guitar strings and rollie papers and chucking them on Jack and Sanjay's unmade beds. Restacking vinyls. Picking up wrappers. Jack would say the house already has a mummy.

Goes back to his iPad but can't concentrate on the American dude tic-tacking up the gap between two San Franciscan office buildings. Picks up his phone; no messages: no extra shift needs urgent filling. Sanjay and Jack both at uni. The shapeless hours that belonged to him, that were his to waste, have grown horns.

He pauses, loose and limber, in the corridor and rubs his palms in a circular motion. They are like cowhide. He has that feeling of old: whipped up, like something is about to split open. Cusses and kicks at the broken bit of skirting board but it doesn't help.

Late afternoon is peak hour below the rail bridge—a jam of kids in mussed uniforms hurling rocks and kissing and smoking and fighting, drinking cold sweets out of cardboard cups—but needs must. Joe stands at the kitchen sink and drinks two full glasses of water then pulls on his cheap Chinese Feiyue. The kung-fu shoes are almost worn through but he likes them like that. It's the next best thing to no shoes at all.

Out the door; key tucked between two bricks. Stretching up through his spine and then higher, onto the balls of his feet, straight as a stringer, before returning heels to ground. Rising and falling repeatedly, without teetering, then dropping down, still balanced on his forefeet, into a slow squat and smoothly back up. Standing in neutral, still and quiet, five long measured breaths in which he remembers—everything, before clearing the low brick fence in a running jump. Precision landing, right foot swivelling left. Swerving around woman with pram; dash to corner.

Sharp right towards the playground, clearing the rail with a speed vault. Swinging glibly along the monkey bars then bounding up the yellow slide pausing for less than a decimal point at the top before dropping down the other side onto the spongy play surface into a roll into a sprint up the footpath south past the sweatshops to his favourite laneway. A climb-up onto the concrete wall then *quadrupedie* crawl—cat balance— along the narrow wall before dropping down into a straight, hard run, until his head has cleared and he is at the bridge.

The kids are on the northern side so he takes the south. There is less here to train with but he needs to get close to the ground, so for a time he scrambles up and down the metal-grated stairway on his hands and feet; forwards down, backwards up. He does it as softly as he can, feeling each movement surge through his body, every muscle and tendon. He is barely there, barely human. Then he moves to the pillar with the slight incline and the six bolt ends protruding some twelve feet up, to practise his *passe muraille*. He's still a couple of feet short of the bolts but he does five, ten, fifteen wall runs. Starting some twenty feet back each time, spitting onto his hands to wet the soles of his shoes, long strides in the approach and a final running jump at the wall, right foot first, pushing up, reaching with his torso. He knows he will touch the bolts some day. It is only a matter of time.

Spent, he drops to the ground, drenched in sweat, panting, and lets himself go limp, skin melting into the hard cool surface of the concrete. He lies there for a while, sensing sweetly where his body ends and the concrete begins, then rises slowly and makes a final cat leap onto the side of the platform beneath the southern end of the bridge. Takes the envelope of tobacco out of his pants and rolls a cigarette.

Lights up then gazes along the symmetrical inner workings of the bridge—so high above the water—sizing up the beams and stringers, the bracing and struts.

It won a design award, this bridge; they said it was 'cool' and 'grand'. The decorative holes along its brash orange sides suggest Swiss cheese. But Joe likes it for its newness—the planning sign still planted in the ground. The bridge holds no memories. It is simply a giant climbing frame, brand-spanking, with a nice mix of footholds, handholds and sheer drops. And aside from the kids who hide out between school and home, it is almost always empty. Trains rattle over, fat carp harry below, but the underside is his.

When he pulls up outside the laundromat, the sun is dropping from the sky. He ducks into the machine room, already brightly lit ahead of the night shift. A man in a hoodie is stretched out along three orange plastic seats, sleeping soundly, smelling slightly of decay. Joe pulls the room ad off the corkboard advertising cello lessons and tarot readings and panel beating; scrunches it, and tosses it in the bin.

Indrah is agitated, more than is her wont at half past eleven on a Thursday morning. She is patrolling the fence that separates the enclosure from the sleeping quarters, ploughing a track in the dry dirt. It is not her usual pacing but something more heightened. Every few minutes she emits a low growl, not dissimilar to the sound of an engine warming—an old Ford GT, in need of a tune. Did she not get enough horse for breakfast? Is she pissed off with her brothers? It is unusual for her to vocalise and Elise wishes, again, that she might understand the tiger's meaning.

It's a vanity to want this. If the cat is prisoner here, what does that make her? Voyeur? For tens of thousands of years, hominids and tigers occupied separate territories, divided the earth and respected the borders, until the past devastating century when the human project got out of hand. Now more tigers inhabit cages than jungles and so Elise sits on this chilly morning in this decent zoo, the leafless plane trees like great wooden hands petitioning the clouds, bearing witness to Indrah's distress.

Each week, at the same time, she comes. Reposes on the long wooden bench facing the moat at the front of the enclosure and stays an hour, rain or shine. Sometimes she wears a coat, a navy full-length hooded number she picked up at the army surplus that doubles as disguise. On the way in, each Thursday, she fills her keep-cup with sweet black coffee from Meerkat Manor, sometimes buying a bone-light coconut cookie from the jar on the counter. Occasionally she jots ideas and sketches in a notebook or does a crossword or sends a work email on her phone. But mostly she sits and watches, keeping distant, obscure company with the cats. Sometimes the hour passes and she can't remember a thing.

No one knows that she does this, not her husband, son, or her best friend. It is a private sacrament. She cannot give it up.

And each week is different. Today the place is subdued— whole stretches of minutes without a single passer-by. Earlier, though, a blonde mother strolled through with her two blonde toddlers. 'Ooh, a tiger,' she told them, giving them a name for their primal fear. 'Listen to its growl!' Elise studied the small faces, so undefended in their horror and delight, and it was enough to make her want to go home and weep.

Her hour is coming to a close and, as if in acknowledgement, Indrah moves into the stand of bamboo and drops gracefully to lying, surrendering to the groundhog day fate of her existence. Elise leaves her satchel on the bench and walks to the second of the two glass viewing-panes, rests her forehead against the cold surface. The tiger is so startlingly beautiful she could be a coked-up supermodel: the bored demeanour; the unpredictability; those crazy stripes daubed over her jack-o'-lantern fur and soft white underbelly; stiletto talons that could release your soul before you've had time even to yelp.

'You okay?' Elise murmurs stupidly. 'What was happening in there today, gorgeous?'

Indrah ignores her. Elise glances around; there is no one watching. She lifts her palms to the glass, spreads them, keeps whispering. It's an incantation. 'I wish you could tell me. Trapped in there. No way out. Your big wild heart.'

The tiger seems to settle further into herself, dropping her head onto her front paws in an audible release. And as if she too can now make peace with the day, Elise collects her stuff and walks out, past the otters and the lemurs, to her bike chained to the rack outside. Already looking towards next week, when she will be back.

They are lying on the roof at midnight in their coats and beanies while Sanjay labours downstairs, stoned, on an overdue assignment.

'So what did you want to be before you decided to throw your life away?' Jack says.

'That's harsh.'

Jack laughs.

'Don't tousle my hair.'

'I love you. You don't *care*. You're above and beyond.'

Joe ponders this observation, how banal it is and how far off. 'I make a wage.'

'You do more than I do. For sure. You work harder. You are a better person.'

Joe doesn't respond.

'I'm thinking of transferring to Law.'

Joe turns his head to look at his friend in the moonlight. 'Huh.'

'Well? What do you think?'

'Yeah, I can see that. I can see you pulling precedents out of your top hat. That's cool.'

'My dad doesn't think I'm smart enough.'

'You're smarter than him. No offence to your father. Who is very nice.'

'No he's not.' They laugh. 'Anyway, nothing I do is going to make that man happy . . . What about you, Joe? What is your heart's desire? Pretend for a moment you have no compunction.'

'I don't think my heart's desire is the point.'

'Then what is?'

'I don't know. Endurance.'

'That's *it*? In your "one precious life"?' Jack mimics Sanjay. 'That's your meaning?'

'What more do you think I need?'

Jack groans. 'You have so much going for you. You got the looks, the brains. You work like an arsehole and for what? I don't get it, that's all.'

'Give me a fucking break. Just because you never know what you want.'

'I'm sorry. Too many beers. I'm just saying. It's tough love. You know you are my hero.'

'Shut up.'

'You know that.'

Silence and stars. And then after some minutes, Jack snores. Joe kicks him. 'Go to bed.'

''Kay, Mum.' Jack slides off the roof, fumbles down the ladder, pisses against the lemon tree, pulls the back door shut.

Joe is sober, though, and wide awake. A tram hurtles by on High Street heading to the depot. A steady but thin stream of cars, occasionally pausing, engines idle, at the pedestrian crossing that leads to the 7-Eleven. He tunes into a heated conversation between a couple at the laundromat next door but can't make out the words.

The stars are showing off tonight. Look at me! And me! Aren't I just the thing! He thinks of her: the girl. What was it about her? Her green eyes and catlike containment. He pictures her in the kitchen, facing him with her arms crossed, the challenge in her eyes, her body. His breath catches and he feels himself harden. It's been there all week: hunger, like a low-level virus. He wants to reach up into the sky and draw her down.

But he stops and breathes out. One thing he has never lacked is willpower.

2

Friday evening he runs to work. Showers out back then pulls on the requisite black jeans and t-shirt from a locker still covered in graffiti from whatever high school offloaded it. Ties on the short black canvas apron; he is the grim reaper of tabletops. In the staffroom mirror, one of those two-dollar-shop numbers with strip lighting so you can make out like you're a showgirl, he runs his hands through his mop of dark hair and stares into his mother's olive eyes. Sees her own wariness there and knows he should call her. Knows he won't. He comes from a line of owls.

He makes coffee and thinks about the nurse. When she arrived last night after dark with her boxes he had that queasy sensation again, of minutes and lifetimes summarily spliced. He offered to help and she scowled—'Yeah, no, I've got it'—and he could have sworn he'd seen that look before.

So while she heaved her way into their house, one carton at a time, he sat in an armchair in the living room looking at parkour clips on YouTube. One in particular—a guy on a rooftop in Tokyo making an eleven-foot cat leap to a twin tower. The span of the gap and the drop would stretch the most elite *traceur*, but every time he watches the clip he feels his own heart fly across the divide, imagines his body travelling with the same power and abandon.

After she'd finished moving in, the nurse went to her room, closed the door and did not rematerialise until he heard her leaving for work. So he happened into the lean-to on the way to the clothesline. Spying, actually, seeing as the rotary line creaking in the night breeze was hung only with Sanjay's damp overalls, and he had to push open her door. He switched on the bare globe and stood in the middle of the room to size her up. A wooden rack hung with clothes, at least half navy blue—uniform, probably. A cast-iron plant in a metal pail; one of those creatures you cannot kill, no matter the neglect. Double mattress on the floor made up with faded stripy linen and coarse grey blankets. A pile of books leaning against the wall—some novels, *Mosby's Dictionary of Medicine, Nursing*

& Health Professions, a high-school poetry text. A cheap lamp and a postcard pinned to the wall above the bed reproducing an old black-and-white photo of a city, somewhere in Europe maybe, with a church, a bridge, a lone figure. Somewhere she has been or would like to go?

He drank it all up and, for no good reason, thought, *I know you*, and, *You're trouble.*

It's just under an hour till bar opening so Joe polishes cutlery, really just to get it looking clean. There is a spoken-word event tonight and the woman who made the booking promised a crowd, suggesting scant attendance. He has to work this room and the main one, so when he's done with the knives and forks he wanders around straightening chairs, wiping up crumbs, lighting candles in blue glass jars. He likes this part of the night: stage set, players yet to walk on. He likes stirring up the stale but ever-expectant air—sorry and glad in equal measure that hopes for transcendence are rarely met. There will be an exchange of bread and wine for money and then people will go back to their workaday lives.

And so the night transpires. The public bar fills and fifty-odd show for the event. He is in and out and back and forth with fresh sardines and bowls of warmed olives, artisan pizza and wedges of beetroot chocolate cake. At the halfway mark, he walks through the smaller function space and a man is reading a prose poem about the Second Coming. Joe glances around the room and notes there could be a dozen Jesuses in here, tugging their thoughtful beards, bemused by the prophet before them.

In the short lulls between short orders, Joe hangs out with the chef Lena in the kitchen. Skater girl with a Ukrainian lilt and Cossack-blue eyes. Hands like threshers. When he's hungry she makes him a bowl of spaghetti with garlic and chilli that he wolfs down, standing by the stove. Later he sneaks her a half-bottle of red. They talk shit and make each other laugh, leavening the hours.

When the last punter has stumbled forth on this night like any other, Joe helps Lena finish up, wrapping the great block of butter, wiping down the fridge; a final load of the dishwasher that fills the kitchen with hot lemony steam. The cleaners arrive, a husband-and-wife team, and Joe is heading back to the change room when Lena asks if he wants to go for a drink.

He shrugs. 'I don't drink.'

'You drink coffee, right? So come.'

'Yeah . . . okay. Cool.'

They change out of their sweaty, smoky garb. Lena takes a baguette and tub of olives and puts them in her bag, wedging her battered skateboard under her left arm. They walk out into the Fitzroy night.

A couple of blocks north is a little all-nighter where there is always a game of cards in play. They order coffee, and grappa for her, and she unties her hair. She sighs as she does it: the chorus of a billion workers kicking off their boots. Her hair is long and straight and tawny like honey too long in the hive. He's never really looked at it before—she always has it tied up or under some psychedelic scarf—and he notices how attractive she is away from the flush and bustle of the kitchen. She has a tiny gap between her front teeth and an economy of movement, like her body is saving itself for bigger things. For an instant he is sorry he doesn't feel something more for her—he thinks she might like that. But it is better this way.

As if reading his mind, she shakes her head. 'You are a bad man, Joe.'

'So you've got me all figured out.'

'No. But you're interesting.'

'You must be bored.'

She sighs; stretches her arms up and back, lengthening her neck. 'A little. It's cold. Everyone's heading indoors to watch TV. I've got no money—can't fly north to the sun. And, you know, I'm halfway to fifty and I haven't made anything to keep.'

'I didn't realise you were so old.'

She laughs. 'What are you? Twelve?'

'Twenty-two.'

'Just a baby.'

'I thought I was a bad man.'

'Same thing.'

'Well, you've still got time to make your mark. I'm sure it'll be worth the wait.'

'Ha. Thanks.'

She knocks her glass against his cup and they break bread—the barista doesn't care—and make a mess of the table. They bitch about Boss and the price of living. She tells him about her cat who keeps getting into fights and her depressive father who plays the trumpet. Which leads to a long story about her paternal grandparents' forced exile from Kyiv and their two years' indentured labour on the Snowy Mountains Hydro-Electric project, where they worked from dawn till dusk, quartered in separate camps. Lena's grandad had to get a special dispensation to visit his son—Lena's father—on the day of his birth. Which leads to the politics of irrigation and the renewed spectre of drought; diminishing world water. He is not always sure where they are going but it is inconsequential. They are easy with each other; she is like a big sister to his only child.

When the clock strikes three, she stands up and yawns. 'I like you, Joe,' she says, as if something has been decided. Then, 'See you on the job.' She throws money on the table and walks out, drops her board and skates off down the dark street.

He is smiling as he sets off in a light run towards home. There is little traffic. A couple is curled up back to back in a tram shelter under a carefully laid doona of newspaper. A lone mutt walks east with intent. A few late-night revellers holler as he overtakes them.

As he approaches the house he looks for a sign of the nurse, but the lean-to is dark.

Her parents said they were going too fast; it wasn't natural at their age. This was the time to be young and irresponsible—or at least, her father qualified, without significant responsibilities. He did a lot of this verbal self-editing, her father, and staccato throat-clearing—sometimes mid-sentence—like he was imparting a hidden message in Morse code. Probably a device he employed to unsettle witnesses in his substantial job, or perhaps just the fags he filched when her mother wasn't looking. He worked long hours at his firm and Jen could do perfect imitations of his yard-long stare. She was often angry with him—until he was actually there at the bench in their warm kitchen, drinking some fine wine, all rugged cleft-chinned thoughtfulness, and then all she wanted was his approval. He gave it to her in single stems.

Probably he saw Joe as a rival—some oedipal thing. But with time they seemed to accept that Joe loved her like they did. They stopped treating him like an error and slowly welcomed him into their storybook lives. He attended her great-aunt's eightieth birthday tea at the RACV club; he and Jen got cosy in the disabled toilet. He drank boutique beers and barbecued swordfish with her dad in their pretty backyard. He played Xbox with the older brother while Jen did homework—always so conscientious; her mum appearing at perfect moments with snacks and cool drinks. He could have stayed there forever.

But he didn't love her like they did: he loved her more. That first year, they hardly saw their friends. They went to the local pool just so they could paddle at opposite ends and watch each other from a distance. They lay on the crackly yellow grass in the park near her house and he told her ghost stories until she'd want to be held. They had sex whenever and wherever they could. Once under a weeping willow beside the Merri Creek; once on a country train during a school excursion. Mostly in one of their bedrooms, on the floor, against the door, with the music turned up. Until her parents cottoned on and had heart-to-hearts with them both, separately; ringing his mother to discuss it further and finally giving their tacit, reluctant approval, knowing there was fuck-all else they could do. In a state of near-constant arousal, they were rarely apart, and if they were, the ache was intolerable.

His mother was never worried. She had always left him to get on with it—life—and anyway, she loved Jen at first sight. Within weeks of Joe bringing her home, the two of them were taking walks together, coming back with soft faces and private jokes. Jen would bring over fancy groceries and make tacos or blancmange. She enjoyed his mother's Joni Mitchell and cheap Chilean wine. She liked being at his house more than her own: the freedom of it, the lack of supervision. She could play at being an adult. At her house, he realised later—after—he got to be a child.

I don't just love you, I want to be you, she told him once. They were walking home from school, early autumn, holding hands. She had new blue boots that had made her inexplicably sad. It was like that with Jen—things hurt her in ways he didn't understand, and it could all change in a breath. Sometimes he felt like he was competing with the spectacle going on inside her head. He needed cue cards but he had to ad lib.

This ugly face?

I'm not kidding.

He waited for her to get it out.

You don't care what other people think. You're as good as you are. And you're beautiful.

He remembers he laughed. *I want to be me so that I can have sex with you.*

You're not listening, she said. She pulled ahead, hefting her bag which was overloaded with maths and chemistry.

What did I do? he stopped and shouted after her. *What?*

I'm sure you'll figure it out.

He caught up and pulled her into a tight embrace. Big man. You *are beautiful. I'm just lucky.* He remembers the feeling of her face tucked into his neck, the wet of her tears. He remembers his desire, his stupidity, his chronic unconcern. He took it all for granted, every waking minute.

If he could go all the way back. To the footpath near the milk bar where they bought hot potato cakes and smoked stolen cigarettes. He would tell her to find someone better. Someone who could actually look after her. He'd have told her to run for her life.

———

Tuesday morning, when Adam has left for work, Elise starts the bread. Mixes up the sticky dough of flours—white and rye, water, salt, seeds, and a dollop of sour starter from the jar on the counter. Kneads for ten minutes or so, turning it inside out, over and over, this stodge that sustains them. Puts it back into the bowl and throws a damp tea towel over; places the bowl on the floor near the heater. She'll be working that dough all day.

Her marriage is critically injured and this is life support—the things they do to keep the heart of the house beating. The money he brings in. Stems of wild orchids on anniversaries, like troupes of tiny golden ballet dancers. The way he might sometimes iron her pyjamas when he is doing his shirts in front of the TV. The food she prepares. Vegetables from the garden. The clean surfaces. Red wine. Footy season. Long, silent hours of reading their way into other existences, side by side. But there can be no new beginnings—this is their disease: there is only ever after. Still, she cannot imagine them apart: with one another they need never explain. They can live it out wordlessly, this second half of their lives.

She warms the last of the coffee in the pot and sets up her laptop at the kitchen table, a forty-eight-year-old graphic designer in a cyber-world full of brilliant and cheap young talent. She has a few loyal clients who know she can work to a brief, deliver on time, and occasionally come up with something perfectly bewildering. Those are the jobs she likes—clients confident enough to risk confusion on the road to enchantment. And though plenty of her work is colour-by-numbers, it is probably here that there are still shades of the person she was. When she sits down with a new brief, and the house is quiet and there is time enough, she can still find something that needs to be expressed and she lets herself have it.

For the current job she has to come up with a new look for an organic cosmetic line. Their image is too squelchy and they want something spare that still carries an echo of earth. She works for an hour or so, bringing up different images and palettes; looking up half-remembered quotes to follow thoughts to more thoughts. Something starts to pulse but is still formless.

She closes the laptop, kneads the dough, and then gets out her pad and pencils. Sketches a woman looking down to a point some metres ahead, a picture of calm contemplation; behind her, a raging sea; an inexorable tide. Nah. Too overwrought. Depressing. Screws it up and throws it across the room. Sketches the trunk of the woman again in quick firm lines, this time holding the sea, an ocean of rippling waves, cupped in her hands. She looks smug—and it's too fanciful. Then, without thinking, on the next blank sheet she starts to draw a cat. Carelessly at first, with the lightest of strokes, then with growing purpose, a tiger takes shape. She watches it stretch out languidly across the paper. Stripes appear; felid eyes gaze up at her. She notices her heart is racing as time itself slows to a crawl.

When the doorbell rings she startles. Tears the paper from the pad and, on a whim, deposits it high up in the linen closet at the end of the corridor. No doubt she will happen upon it one day and dispose of it properly.

A courier with a recycled-cardboard box. She signs his digital release then unpacks cosmetic samples onto the kitchen table. Another fit of kneading and more sketching for the job, with a row of lipsticks uncapped before her. For lunch, a warmed-up bowl of leftovers in the sunroom overlooking the gnarly old apricot tree, with its stubble of yellow leaves that refuse to join their fallen comrades.

She remembers another autumn. How as soon as she started breastfeeding at the rickety garden table, comfortably settled with her newspaper and glass of water, her toddler son would climb the apricot tree, right up to the very top, and then ask her to help him down. She would feel like a fat fly wrapped tight in these sticky strands of love and need, and she might, in those moments, dream of being elsewhere, alone and unimpeded. Sometimes she would pluck the baby off mid-suck and let her howl on a rug on the grass while she climbed up there to get him. Other times she would talk him down, as if from a ledge, offering bribes or threats, intoning that idiotic rule: If you can get yourself up, you can get yourself down again.

She remembers gazing at her baby's profile once they had resettled. Eyes lightly closed, as if only pretending; cheeks working in and out, little gulping sounds; a sweep of soft dark hair on her small perfect head. Entirely safe she was, then: thriving. She remembers the screech of rainbow lorikeets in the almond tree whose roots were later destroyed by a plumber. The radio singing out in vain from the kitchen.

And now she sits in the sunroom with her empty bowl laced with grains of rice, halfway through a day, longing for impediments and impossible demands.

———

Faint knock, almost imperceptible.

It is just before dawn and he is awake—couldn't sleep. Didn't have to work last night so went to bed early in order to toss and turn like a fuckwit. Ended up playing on the iPad and tracking the movements of the seven-legged huntsman on the ceiling. The spider has been travelling from room to room for months, spending a few weeks on one ceiling before moving on, like some restless nomad looking for the good grass.

'Come in.' He is expecting Jack with an insurmountable life problem.

She opens the door and edges in, the nurse. She is wearing navy blue scrubs and black rubber clogs, a lurid yellow stethoscope hanging around her neck like a piece of fairground jewellery. She's got pins in her hair that serve only to emphasise its scruffiness. No makeup on those beautiful, relentless eyes.

'Sorry,' she says, 'I heard you yawning. You sounded like a gibbon.'

'Thanks.' He sits up against the bedhead, arms crossed over his bare chest. He's naked under the doona and feels both vulnerable and ridiculous. Every time he talks to her he seems to strike these dandy poses.

'I just got home from work. Wanted to ask you a favour.'

'Mmm?' All studied nonchalance.

'I can't open the windows in my room. Any of them.'

'Oh.' He glances towards his own window. Frowns. 'It's cold.'

'I know. But I can't sleep without fresh air. I've actually been trying to open them for days.'

'Hang on. Give me a minute.'

She retreats and he pulls on tracksuit pants and a t-shirt. Pads down the corridor and into the lean-to.

'Yeah, I don't know when we would have last opened these. This room has been empty as long as I've been here.'

He yanks hard at one of the levers. Nothing. Tries another. They are definitely not moving. Rusted together and then sealed with a coat of paint during Vijay's last clean-up.

'I feel stupid asking. Sorry. I've been lifting oversized men in and out of their sickbeds all night but these windows . . .'

'Yeah I can see. Let me get something.'

He goes to his room. He's got an old metal ruler somewhere, from high school. He finds it buried under a pile of stuff on the desk his uncle gave him that was meant to be *for* something.

Back in her room, she is sitting on the edge of the mattress, rubbing her bare white feet. She is almost luminous in this dark grey light and he pauses, looking down at her. He wants to cross the wild plains of the tiny room, get on his knees; take off her uniform—slowly. He wants to get under the frayed old blankets and warm her.

'What about the sun?' he asks as he's jimmying open one of the levers. 'It doesn't keep you awake?'

She points to a tatty airline eye mask on the pillow. 'Earplugs too.'

He manages to open all four windows and icy air comes streaming in, like river water.

'Can I make you a cup of tea or something?' she asks.

'No. Thanks. I can't really see the point of tea.'

She smiles. 'Me neither. I was trying to make a good impression—the day you interviewed me.'

'By not drinking the tea I made you?'

'Well, I got the room.'

'Felt more like I was going for the job.'

'You did well.' She is grinning, looking up at him. 'Hey, Joe—thanks.' The way she says his name; the way she holds him with her eyes like she knows him and understands. He is riveted.

They both grow very still, watching one another. He has to get out of there. 'Enjoy your fresh air.'

'I notice you run,' she says to his back. 'Maybe we could go together sometime?'

'I go at odd times,' he says over his shoulder, not meeting her eyes.

'As you can see, I keep odd times too.'

'Sure. Let's run some time.' He closes the door firmly behind him. Goes to his room and puts the ruler back on his desk.

The others are still asleep. 'Fuck,' he murmurs under his breath. 'Get a grip.' Eats a bowl of Weet-Bix in the living room, looking out the window at the garbage truck; its jerky motorised arm is picking up the bin, lifting, emptying, replacing. He thinks of the nurse lifting grown men in and out of their sickbeds, her thin lovely arms. He imagines her lying there, metres away, right here right now. *She is right here right now.*

Goes to his room and pulls on his magic shoes. He has to be at his second job at the cafe up the road in forty-five minutes. Not time for the bridge but a quick detour. He steps outside, deposits the key, pounces.

3

Sunday afternoon he borrows Sanjay's car to pick up Deck. It's a rusty little black Citroen that takes a long time to warm up, a hand-me-down from Vijay. There is a ten-centimetre naked rubber lady hanging from the rear-view mirror that squeaks if you press her middle. The car smells like dope and spice; the car smells like Sanjay.

He has been meeting Deck for a year and a half now, fortnightly, but he still gets fidgety before he sees him. Like he should have combed his hair or said his prayers or got a real job—been someone a little more responsible. There's always a bassline of fear, playing low and steady, that somehow he will fail him.

In the beginning they would go to cafes. Deck would order two coffees at once then chain-smoke and stare at the traffic. He said he didn't really see the point of being there but that he would come to keep his mum happy. He'd just returned home after six months in care. Sometimes he ordered chocolate cake and ate it with his fingers, sucking the icing off each one. It could feel, to Joe, like looking the wrong way down a telescope at his own teenaged self. He couldn't really see the point either. But he had committed to twelve months with this mentoring program in a rash of life choices that followed his sobering up.

They tried movies. That was better. There was a gradual gentling, side by side, in the dark space. They could laugh more freely and stop trying to impress one another, learning to take comfort in knowing they had both turned up again. They saw some really shit movies. After that a brief swing of golf, of all things, because he'd got a freebie from a customer. They did that three times.

Then a couple of months ago they were sitting beside a park, smoking, and there were some young guys playing soccer, using Coke bottles for goalposts. They were invited to join. Since then they've been taking a ball to the park every second Sunday. A couple of hours go by and they don't say much but it feels good. He thinks the soccer thing could last a while.

He picks Deck up from outside his unit, and they head to Coburg Lake. It's going to rain but fuck it. Joe has packed a cooler bag with sausages, bread and sauce.

'How's school?' He can feel the boy rolling his eyes. 'You're rolling your eyes.'

'You always have to ask. School sucks. You know it does. You said so yourself.'

'Did I?' He glances across. Deck has grown his fringe and lately he speaks with his head down, eyes peering up through this ridiculous nut-brown curtain. He's got a little disco of acne across the bridge of his nose. Joe remembers being rude. He remembers.

'Yeees. You hated it.'

They both laugh. 'Yeah, and as I have *also* said, smartarse, I'm the living proof that you should work hard and go to university and make something of yourself.'

'Now you sound like my English teacher. All the same shit. Me? University? LOL.'

'Give me three reasons why not.'

'Good. For. Nothing.'

'That's just fucking stupid.'

'No need for the bad language.' They pull into the car park. 'Anyway, why don't you go to university if it's so good?'

'Maybe I will.'

'Okay, so we can go together, and I'll hold your walking stick while you pee.'

At the oval they run a few laps then play kick to kick, juggling and passing the ball back and forth with their feet. Another hour of goalies-up.

They stand undercover at the barbecues, grilling sausages as it starts to rain.

'I aced a maths test,' Deck offers.

Joe nods, pretends to be unimpressed. 'I was okay at maths.'

'And there's a girl who really likes me.'

'Oh yeah?'

'Yeah. How could she help it?'

'How could she, my arse.'

———

Job done. Late Sunday afternoon, she sends it off and starts her completion clean. It is a personal punctuation mark. This time it was ten days between sweeps; sometimes it's more. What counts is the ritual—containment of the universe, of callous time, to a cupboard full of green cleaning products.

She turns up The Go-Betweens and vacuums then mops. Sluices the toilets. Wipes dust from the open shelves that cover two walls of the living room. After, she cuts roses from the garden and puts them in a bowl on the dining-room table.

Adam is out playing squash so she puts another record on the turntable and opens a beer, gets out her sketchpad. There are five tigers now—clandestine cats lurking in the linen closet. She is still playing around with the last, using pastels this time. The arrival of colour is a leap, an investment; she knows she is being drawn in deeper but pretends she is not. With each tiger she has reached a point where there is nothing to add or take away yet none feel finished. She can't work out what is missing.

Adam's car in the driveway. She quickly packs the paper and materials away.

Key in the lock: a perfect fit but it grates.

She remembers listening for the key in the early hours of the morning during her children's high-school years. She could never sleep until her babies were home. Her best friend Jill, who chose not to have children, would tell her to loosen her scarifying grip. But each time the children were safely returned, however drunk and inconsiderate, banging around the kitchen making jaffles at three in the morning, was a reprieve.

Adam comes in, flushed, throwing keys into the fruit bowl. Leans down and kisses her.

'Did you win?'

They follow their script.

'Nup.' He stoops to get a beer out of the fridge. 'I'm going to shower. We should watch the match.'

He walks back up the corridor, his t-shirt darkened with sweat; strong brown legs. He is handsome—and human—but she feels nothing for him at all.

So she makes an omelette. Goes out into the dusk garden and picks fresh herbs. Beats the eggs, grates hard cheese, chops chilli and parsley and mushrooms. Warms the pan with butter.

Tosses a salad.

Serves the simple meal.

And here he is, down again in a clean tracksuit, so neat, opening wine, collecting the cutlery. And for an instant she sees something young in his face. And then it is gone. And it wasn't, anyway, for her.

His mind is on a case so she knows he will be hard to engage. It has always been his out—work. She wonders if he's noticed how long it has been since she tried to break in, or if it's all the same to him.

He pours them each another drink and they sit in front of the TV, side by side. After they've eaten, he rests a hand on her leg and speaks to the umpire. Perhaps he is really speaking to her? 'Poor decision.' 'Not even close!' 'About time.' 'You fucking moron.'

After the match he goes to his study to keep working. She fiddles on her iPad for a while, looking at Facebook updates, then goes to bed to dream about tigers.

—

The bridge is deserted when he pulls up breathless from a hard run late on Wednesday afternoon. He takes the northern end and starts with sets of push-ups, sit-ups, lunges, slow squats till everything is burning and he can no longer feel the separate parts, only the whole.

Needs to focus on balance conditioning. There are two strips of old rail laid in a decorative wedge on the gravel alongside a low concrete wall. For a while he walks slowly back and forth along the rails, one foot in front of the other, maintaining control and precision, minimising sway. Back and forth. It's child's play but he gives it his full concentration. Then, balancing crossways on the rail on the balls of his feet, he lowers into a crouch before rising again to stand, engaging stabilisers in the lower legs. To bring in his arms, some *quadrupedie* along the narrow surface, slippery and cold, hands and feet moving in feline symmetry, forwards the length; backwards; side to side. Again. Again.

Then a bunch of pop-ups on the low concrete wall. Placing his hands on the wall a couple of feet apart, precision jump to land feet between his hands. Reversing the movement. Doing it again. He needs a rail to progress it.

Stretches for a bit, muscles hot and sore, then squats on the gravel and gazes along the creek as it travels west—its castor-brown waters swallowed up by the overhanging willows a few hundred metres downstream. Behind the overhang is the old wooden footbridge, just out of sight. He comes here several times a week but never runs beyond this point. It is not that he is afraid of what he might feel at the footbridge but that he wants to preserve it just as it was.

He has a notion, though. Jogs to the end of the rail bridge and swings up and onto the orange steel girder. Easy to shuffle sideways along the fifteen-centimetre ledge. In a few minutes he is nearing the centre. It is a long drop to the straggle of water. He pauses there, looking down, and things become so beautifully simple: you live or you die.

He is in a position now, looking out through one of the cheese holes, to see abstract patches of the footbridge mosaicked with foliage. He looks down again and whistles. Fuck it. To be up here; to look down. To see that place from a distance, where he gave himself over. It is terrifying and somehow just right.

How would the falling feel? Would it go fast?

Then a rumbling—coming closer. Train. A bolt of panic. Makes himself weightless and still, resting lightly against the girder. The train roaring overhead, just metres above, the whole structure trembling. Must not close his eyes. Or look up. Must not breathe. Or sweat so much that he slides off this thing. The train is over. He exhales. Laughs. Legs loose with fear.

And then he is distracted by the pillar across from him, on the other side of the train line. His brain is doing calculations before he is even conscious of it. The gap would be at least nine feet. From standing, the top of the pillar is roughly chest-high, so it would have to be a cat leap. There is a nice concrete horizontal surface for his fingers to grab.

The ledge he is standing on is too narrow to push off from his forefeet without first resting heels up against the vertical surface. Shit. Once engaged, there would be no turning back. And supposing he pulled it off, the leap, then a quick mount onto the top of the pillar and *lache*—monkey arms—back along a joist to this side. The distance is achievable; it's not a world-class jump. But if he stuffed it he would be carp bait.

Making the assessments has calmed his nervous system. He sidles back along the girder to the end of the bridge and jumps down onto the gravel, soft as a cat.

Bollywood is blasting out of the house as he turns the High Street corner. His first thought is of the nurse—is this screechy love shit bothering her? Is she regretting moving in? But she's probably left for work, is hardly part of the household anyway with the hours she keeps.

He slams the front door behind him and Sanjay emerges from the living room in a towel, wriggling his hips. 'Joey! Brother! We have been awaiting your arrival with great eagerness!'

Joe follows Sanjay into the living room where Jack is sprawled on the couch smoking a joint.

'Can we turn down the fucking soap opera?' He lowers the volume on the stereo and perches on a faded velvet armchair to pull off his Feiyue. His socks are drenched with sweat.

'Tonight, we explore the urban wilderness! We will see langur and spotted deer—of course—but also many strange birds with exquisite plumage.' Sanjay is stoned.

'Where is this wilderness of which you speak?' Jack is stoned too.

'There is a national park by the name of Brunswick. This is the famous Brunswick National Park. I have the necessary permit, already fixed. I will be your guide tonight.' When Sanjay is stoned he starts to sound more Mumbai than he really is.

'I say we walk up to the corner and play pool,' Joe says, rubbing his calves. He takes the joint and has a couple of pulls, more to be affable than to get high. Getting high blurs the order of things: he starts to imagine things are just fine.

'Please, do I look to you like a common chinkara? Do you see horns?' Sanjay brushes upwards from his long black ponytail, making horns in the air.

'No, you look like a fucking idiot,' Jack says, laughing, 'but girls love you so I am coming on your trek.'

Joe shrugs. 'Sanjay, I put myself in your expert hands.'

They make toasted cheese sandwiches in Sanjay's frying pan and manage to burn them, distracted by the YouTube clip Joe is showing them of the Tokyo guy on the towers. The kitchen fills with smoke; the sink with dishes; they shower and dress. Eventually they leave the house, going back once for forgotten travel cards and again for beanies.

Joe walks a few beats behind the others, watching them laugh and bounce around the footpath like inflatable car-yard men, arms waving erratically. He tried for a time not to have friends but they come and they get you. When he saw the ad for the room in the house behind the laundromat two years ago he was lost. They didn't interfere or judge as he trampled everything in his path; they didn't applaud when he came to a stop. They were there: he owes them everything. But how not to feel the pull of people you love like vertigo at the edge of a cliff?

They catch a tram then walk the rest of the way into the national park of Brunswick. Sydney Road is full of loud voices, clouds of steamy breath, overcoats. They start at the pool table in the Retreat but Jack and Sanjay are too fucked up to hit the ball.

'Come on, Joe, come on, that one. Over there. In the blue dress. For you.'

'Nah.'

'Are you a man or a eunuch?'

'A uni*corn*, Sanjay. I can only be captured by a virgin.'

He beats them too easily so plays a local shark instead who chews off his arms. That's better.

They move to another bar and then another. Jack and Sanjay are on the prowl, and finally start circling some girls, young, maybe even high school. Joe hangs back but they draw him in. One of the girls is wooing him. She is sweet, talking about the barista course her brother once did after he mentions he works in a cafe. He steers her towards Jack and excuses himself, goes outside to smoke.

He is thinking about leaving when he sees Lena crossing the street. All straight-from-work, hair bunched up, short leather jacket. She sees him and veers over.

'Kitchen close early?' he asks as she draws near.

'Uh-huh. Quiet for a Saturday.' She gestures over her shoulder. 'My friend Nadja—and Tim.'

He nods hello.

'You going back in?' she asks, gesturing to the open door.

'Nah, I'm done . . . My friends are hooking up.' He doesn't know why he tells her this; he is glad to see her.

'You don't want to find a lady friend tonight?'

He smiles. 'Not tonight. I just want my bed.'

'Your bed. Are you flirting with me?'

'No.' He laughs.

'These two want to play but I am fucking beat, and I burnt my arm on the grill again, same spot as last week.' She pulls up her sleeve and shows him the red band on the inside of her wrist.

'Ouch. You should be more careful, Lena.'

She smiles. 'Shall we walk together?'

He texts Sanjay, and Lena says goodnight to her friends. They head east on foot.

'You could do so much better than the bar,' he says. He knows she's worked in decent establishments, places that get blogged and reviewed. 'What are you still doing there?'

'I don't know. It's easy and I'm lazy . . . Maybe I'm scared I'm not really as good as I want to be. One day I'd like to open my own place.'

'Lena's Lounge.'

'First I'd have to win the lottery or marry a millionaire.'

'I'm sure you could pull that off.' They walk a bit. 'What made you want to cook for people anyway?'

She pauses on the street for a moment, as if listening to an echo. 'Okay. Well. The first meal I really remember was stuffed cabbage leaves—*holubsti*. It means "little doves". I was four. I can still see the plate they were on—brown; a coarse dirt-brown plate. And the pale milky green of the leaves folded into a steaming parcel. I was too small to cut it up so my father did that with his big knife and fork. Then the leaves were just these little messy squares. Like life.'

'It sounds sort of disgusting.'

'I ate it up and I knew paradise. Subtle, herby, buttery, the pork was ground in my grandmother's grinder, the rice all plump and separate. It sweated a perfect broth. This was definitely one of the moments that made me.'

'Okay, now it sounds good.'

'I'll make it for you one day.'

'Cool.'

They walk some more in silence.

'So, what's your story then, Joe?' she asks.

'I'm simple, Lena.'

'Bullshit.'

'Make it up if you want. You can give me a back story.'

'*Okay*. Yes. Give me one word—any word—for the beginning.'

'No. You're on your own.' He doesn't really like this game.

'See? This is you all over.'

'Whatever. Okay—carp.'

She laughs. 'Carp? Shit. You might have made it a little easier. It's been a long night.'

They reach a fork in the road. 'Do you want me to walk you home?'

'No, it's not far. I'm a big girl. Hey. My friend Nadja? Her exhibition is opening in a few weeks. Her work is really good. You should come.'

He hesitates; doesn't want to mislead her.

'We are friends, no?'

'Sure.' And he realises he has missed the way girls talk, those meandering streams and sudden depths.

'Then come. You're safe with me.'

He smiles. 'You don't scare me, Lena.'

She shrugs. 'I'm not so sure.'

He watches her drop her board and skate away, and then he runs—onwards, through a landscape that time derides, all the way to the laundromat.

The lean-to is dark; Jack and Sanjay will be gone all night.

He takes a cushion up onto the roof. It is overcast, the sky a vast rolling grey mantle lit by the city. He rolls a cigarette.

"Night, Joe.'

Did he hear that? Maybe she *is* here. Maybe she heard him climbing the ladder outside her room. Was that an invitation? Should he go down there and fall at her feet?

But then there is nothing more and he isn't sure if he imagined it.

4

On Tuesday he works a double shift at the cafe—a hole in the wall on High Street, one of those places with no signage and lots of attitude. A small flowering cactus on each mismatched table. Mellow music, hand-picked, that no one's ever heard of. Probably he wouldn't go there himself but he likes the sisters; they are generous and appreciative bosses. The older one slaps his bottom but he forgives her because she makes vats of moussaka twice a week, and crescent biscuits covered in sugar, and he is allowed to eat as much as he wants.

It's usually busy, too, so there are all those good hours of working and breathing, thinking of fuck-all except when to next flush out the coffee machine and how to improve on his signature star atop the frothy milk. And what time will the old man be in for his cake? Is it the day he plays bowls or the day he sees his adult daughter or one of the other five days when he is simply trying to kill time on the way to his grave? And there is a constant stream of mothers with babies. He smiles at the babies and flirts with the mothers. The day goes.

When he's done the final sluice of the coffee machine and the sisters are polishing the glass cabinets and making up the shopping list—late afternoon hitting their heads like stun guns—he takes his cash and heads out. He is weary right down into his plantar fascia. Taking every shift he can at the bar and cafe but not sleeping much, he has the sense of something gaining on him.

Runs up High Street—past the plastic-surgery clinic attached to the naturopath; the curtain shop and funeral parlour; the tattooist, tobacconist, trendy boutique; the pizza shop and the picture framer; the gun shop right across from the community legal centre—kong vaults a bin and is home: COIN LAUNDRY, red letters on yellow, always OPEN, never too late.

Jack has brought back a tub of his mum's chicken casserole. It's sitting on the counter—obviously too much effort involved in putting it into the fridge. Joe ignores it and slides down the wall till he is sitting on the kitchen floor with his legs stretched out in front of him. He pulls off his runners and moves his feet in circles, flexes and points, kneads the arches with his thumbs. He thinks of the nurse massaging her bare white feet, perched on the edge of her bed. Is it she who is gaining on him? Is this the return of desire?

'You want me to rub your feet, Joey?' Sanjay asks in a high-pitched voice.

'Not even when you say it like that.'

Jack and Sanjay are playing puff soccer, standing either side of the kitchen table blowing a cotton-wool ball between them. Whoever gets it over the opposite side scores a point. They are red in the face with the need to succeed. Joe joins in and for the next hour the three of them rotate at the table. The sun sets.

'Why do you always have to win?' Jack complains to Joe.

'Maybe I'm just better.'

'I've got to start going to the gym again.' Jack lifts his t-shirt and Sanjay makes a groan of disgust. Jack laughs. 'Fuck it, boys, let's eat!'

Joe fills a saucepan with water to cook rice but he can't find the pliers to turn on the stove. They're usually on the counter. He checks through every drawer—twice. Then, for no good reason, wanders down the hall to the lean-to. The door is ajar. He gently pushes it open. The pliers are splayed in the middle of the floor. He is momentarily rattled, but—of course—the windows. That's why his feet brought him here. She's been grappling with the windows again. And there is his ruler, too, on the window ledge. Which means she must have gone into his room when he wasn't there, taken it from his desk. He shakes out the chill that slows his blood, pushes it out through his feet and hands, stretching out his spine reflexively. And how many times has he crossed this threshold in her absence? How many boundaries have already been breached?

He stands in the room, the pliers dangling from his left thumb. It is so cold in here, and he has an overwhelming urge to tidy up. Perhaps he would like to tidy her away. Her blankets are mussed. A discarded uniform lies crumpled at the foot of the bed. He picks it up and puts his face to it and there it is—that faint scent of trees and water.

Did she do this with his things? Could she smell him too?

He takes the pliers back to the kitchen, turns on the stove and pours the casserole into a pan to reheat.

'I did it,' Jack announces, opening beers for himself and Sanjay.

'Well done! But you didn't do it alone.' Sanjay holds up the bottle opener as proof.

'Dickhead. I put the application in—to transfer into Law.'

'Yeah?' Joe says. 'That's cool.' But what he tastes is a tincture of envy. Where did that come from?

'I'm not in yet.' Jack sits at the kitchen table with his guitar, strumming.

'When do you find out?'

'Couple of months.'

'What kind of law you gonna do?' Sanjay chops vegetables for his dinner.

'Criminal. Maybe.'

'*You?*' Sanjay laughs. 'With your record?'

'Fuck off.'

'Wha'? I'm kidding!' Sanjay protests.

'You sound like his old man,' Joe explains. 'What did he say?' Joe asks Jack.

'Doesn't know.'

'Don't tell,' Sanjay says. 'Turn up in five years in a sharp suit. Arrest him!'

Joe smiles but Jack still looks shitty. 'Lawyers don't arrest people, dickhead.'

'True. They just take all their money.'

'You can talk, son of a landlord.'

Sanjay whistles and his knife works the broccoli a little faster. 'Seems to work out for you, *mate*, but, you know, feel free to fuck off.'

Jack picks up his guitar again and starts to play.

Sanjay puts his vegies in the pan with a sachet of readymade dhal from the Indian grocer over the road where he buys his godforsaken three-dollar CDs. He stands and flicks seeds at Jack's back.

'I can feel that.'

'You have the hypersensitivity of a garden snail,' Sanjay notes.

Joe stands between them but he can't be fucked playing den mother tonight. 'I'm going to eat.' He fills a bowl with casserole and goes to the living room to sit in front of the TV.

'This is why we don't cook together,' Jack mutters, following.

'*You* don't cook,' Sanjay calls after him from the kitchen. 'Perry fucking Mason.'

It's late—or early—maybe four am. He is sitting up in bed with the iPad, opening Facebook. He hasn't been in for more than a year: had to wean himself off when he decided to keep living. But he needs to see her.

He's aware there is something of the junkie's ritual about this. The light is off. There is just the low glow of the screen and the sallow moonlight. He's got a fresh packet of tobacco and has lit up, dropping ash into an empty can, breaking house rules. The sashless sash window is wedged open with a shoebox and the cold air cuts through the bullshit. He can see why the nurse likes it; it makes things palpable.

The rest, of course, comes naturally. Logs in and has only to type one letter in the search box for her name to come up.

And then it is opening. And here she is.

'Oh shit,' he groans quietly.

Smiling up at him. So sweetly. So familiar: his familiar. *Wife,* he called her. *Wife, bring me my pipe and finest pair of slippers.*

Her long black hair is caught up in a bunch. She is wearing the red batik dress and you can see the blue straps of her bra. There is sand around her. In the top centimetre of the picture, a strip of muddy green water. Nothing tropical—just St Kilda. Around her shoulders, possessively, a pair of brown arms with the head cut off. His arms. Around her. She is seventeen. Hardly even a number. Just a beginning.

He takes a long punishing suck on his cigarette. He is shivering with cold. He wishes he had a bottle of malt.

There are one hundred and seven photos. He starts the roll of honour, giving each image its due. Can't quail now.

He remembers asking her out for the first time, when they were sixteen. There is no photo of that. They were at school, near the lockers. They'd been burning one another with their eyes for weeks. Messages had been relayed. He asked her if she wanted to go fishing in the Merri Creek. What a smartarse.

We can't eat this, she laughed, after they caught their first carp.

Carp are noxious pests, he explained. *This is community work.*

He'd brought a blanket and a six-pack and they set up beside the low sleeveless footbridge that submerges in big rains. They caught two fat slow fish and he stabbed them right there under the weeping willow, threw them still twitching into the bushes. Big man.

They shared a bag of barbecue chips, and at twilight he moved towards her. Like in a movie—if you could disregard the garbage and the rattle of a passing train. Their first kiss. Was unbelievable. Like something entirely new had announced itself in the world. Your very first taste of ice-cream. The first time you properly catch a wave. Discovering music that sings to you alone. It was unlike any of the other kisses he'd ever won or stolen. They fitted. Mouths. Skin. Their smell. Their taste. From that day, with the dead fish and the beery sunset, maybe it was all foregone.

He scrolls. A photo of her and her friends all dressed up to go to a cocktail party. She is frowning. She didn't want to go. She'd been complaining all week. Then she had a good time. He told her she would. Yawn.

An old photo, scanned, of her with her brother when they were kids, playing outside. They look like storybook children: she's waving a red spade; he's got the bucket. They are pretty much the same child, actually, though she's sporting pigtails.

A dozen photos from school camps. Snaps from a family beach holiday.

There they are, Year 12, with the little girl from up the road who she used to mind on Thursdays after school. They would play Mummy and Daddy, sneaking caresses while the girl watched TV. Jen wanted four children, she said, to make it even. He was going to teach them how to catch and kick.

A photo of them both in t-shirts and undies on the couch at her house, hung-over, saying to her dad, *No, please don't take the picture.* It has been three and a half years since he was in that house that was once a second home.

He is still scrolling when the sun starts to push up its brainless yellow head. 'Fuck off,' he murmurs.

He is beyond tired now. He is angry. Horny. Sad. The way none of this changes but it still feels new; all those chirpy little tags. 'Jen—don't look now!' 'Jen and Nicki feed the lucky ducks.' 'Jen and Joe NYE 2006.'

He hates that she is still here in this pseudo world, only static. He hates that it says where she went to school and what she likes—profiteroles!—and that she never gets to grow up and change—I fucking hate profiteroles! He wishes her parents had just shut the page down.

And then, when he is smoking a last cigarette, readying to log out, he opens his own dormant Facebook page and notices a friend request from someone called Emily Dickinson. For an instant—a skin prickle—he is stunned. Dickinson was Jen's favourite poet; she'd recite stuff when she'd had too much to drink. He didn't pay much attention to the words—too busy stroking her legs. Arsehole.

So without pause he accepts the request. He would accept anything from her. But these instants never last. It is the dawn of another day without her in it, so he drops the iPad to the floor. Heads to the shower.

The rain is soft but steady. She sits huddled on the bench in her overcoat, hood high, satchel tucked beneath her. Thursday, eleven-twenty.

The brothers are out today—Aceh and Hutan. Their sister will be backstage gnawing on a bone. The captive cats are sometimes fed whole carcasses so they can pluck the hairs from lunch first, leaving a little pile of fluff beside the nice clean bones. Their tongues may look like luncheon meat but are in fact covered in tiny barbs used to strip the hide from their prey.

Elise knows. She has been studying. In bed at night, on

her iPad, between work and cyber roaming, she reads about the tigers.

Indrah is the tiger she dreams about but she loves to watch the brothers at play. It is unusual at their ripe old age of four to be enclosed together, but so far fraternal affection has overridden their innate solitary natures. It is a guilty pleasure to watch them lick each other's faces when they should be ripping one another to pieces. Is it because they were born in captivity, like their parents before them, and their parents before them? Are they evolving to fit this new set of circumstances? Despite the zoo's best efforts—the chunks of horse and goat they tie to the tree trunks so the cats will have to climb; the cage rotations so the cats will sniff and spray and try in vain to defend their territories; the moat of green water that they may swim—how can they not be slowly washed of their wildness?

Today, for the first time, Elise has brought a camera. She wanted to capture the tigers for her drawing but the brothers are both at the back of the enclosure under the cover of the trees, skulking. Is the universe telling her something? She sometimes wonders if she should stop this; whatever it is sometimes feels dangerous. And yet sitting here in the rain is going to be the best part of her week. She knows that already.

She hasn't seen Carl in almost two months, though they speak most Sundays. There'll be background noise and sometimes his phone will drop out. Maybe he just hangs up. He has a new girlfriend and they've been going down the coast on the weekends. But long before that: he didn't want to be there in their haunted house. He would stop by on the way somewhere and have a cup of coffee or a beer at the bench, something contained to approximately twenty-two minutes, then light kisses, mutual wishes, for a good night, a good life, and gone. Door closing. She doesn't blame him. He *has* a life, thank Christ.

The rain is easing. She walks to the railing and pushes her hood back, rests her hands on the cold wet metal. She is still trying to tell the brothers apart. Each tiger's stripes are tattooed on their skin—if you shaved them the stripes would remain—and each pattern is unique, like a fingerprint. Elise has spent countless hours playing spot-the-difference, using the photo board beside the enclosure for her game, but she is still unsure who is who. One of the keepers told her once, in passing, that Aceh is the dominant one and Hutan a mama's boy. Probably why they still get on; they've got their roles sorted, no one rocking the cage.

One of the tigers—Hutan?—rubs himself up against the thick trunk of the plane tree, mewls a little, then wanders down to the edge of the water. He sniffs the ground, licks his lips, then stretches, straining his head and neck forwards, his forequarters, his middle, and finally extending his hind legs. He looks up and meets Elise's eyes, as if to garner her reaction to this display, and for several mind-blowing seconds they look into one another's souls. She is transfixed.

Is this why she keeps coming? In the thrall of the tiger's gaze the cage disappears, the zoo falls away, and Elise is as petrified and enraptured as a deer—until the tiger is distracted by a pigeon alighting on a boulder nearby, turning away from Elise before dismissing the bird as too small and flighty to bother with. The world rushes back. Elise is on the right side of the barrier. But she knows that in those fleeting moments he would have had her if he could. Given half a chance, a hole sheared through the wire, the tiger would have delivered her.

Respite from the rain brings a ragtag rush. A school-girl walks past singing 'Eye of the Tiger'; her friend growls. A mother, trying to keep up with her son, smiles over at the big cats: 'Oh, what a darling! Look, Ted! Bye-bye kitty!' A middle-aged Indian couple is in firm agreement that these Sumatrans are not as big or as fine as the Bengals. And a young Maori guy covered in tatts stands at the edge of the barrier, holding up his toddler daughter. 'Whoa,' is all she hears him say. 'Yeeeeah.'

'Yeeeeah,' Elise echoes under her breath, taking out her camera at last.

She takes almost thirty portraits. She is a paparazzo stealing the starlet's soul. The waterside cat stretches out alongside a log by the water. Snap. Cleans his toes. Snap. Amber eyes lazily following a dusky moorhen as it muddles by. Snap. Snap. Eyes closing in a yawn, mouth agape, that huge pink tongue, those teeth! Snap. Snap. Snap.

5

It's a break in protocol: wrong day, wrong time, wrong locale. He told Boss he'd be late, and borrowed Sanjay's car. His hair is still wet from the shower; in black jeans and checked shirt he could be a fucking uni student.

Deck's mum has dressed up too. Tight black t-shirt with a towelling orange butterfly sewn over the left breast; tangerine lipstick. He can see she has never worked hard for attention. Full of spunk, like her son.

He hands her a bag of crescent biscuits from the cafe. It's the first time he's been inside the unit. It's simple and neat. Maybe she tidied for the occasion. There is a vase of short pink roses on the hall table, and one of those bottles of cheap scent with the little sticks poking out.

'You're good for Declan, love,' Marie confides as he follows her down the corridor and into the kitchen at the back. 'He looks forward to your time together.'

Joe smiles. 'Really? I don't know about that.'

Deck's father has shown up, all the way from Lakes Entrance. He knows it's him because of the way his legs are spread in a show of aggressive propriety, his bushman's beard and his scowl, and how Deck is hovering nearby.

Deck's stepdad, with the contrasting shaved pate, is on his phone in the backyard; you can see him pacing through the window. One of the grannies is propped up at the head of the table, clutching with two hands her glass of Coke. There is a chocolate cake with two red-trimmed white candles—1 and 5—ready to light.

'Beer, Joe? Or what about a bourbon?'

'No, thanks.' He notices Deck is holding a beer, though, and so would he have been at fifteen. Still, he would like to knock it from his hands. Instead, he hands Deck an envelope. 'Happy birthday.'

Deck rips it open. Two tickets to an A-league soccer match. Deck grins. 'Yeah, that's cool.'

'You can take a mate if you want. Or your girlfriend.'

Deck looks up drolly from behind his chestnut curtain. 'You'll do.'

'Cool.'

Joe sits down at the table across from Deck's father, who clears his throat in Deck's direction.

'Yeah, thanks,' Deck adds. Then to his dad, 'This is Joe, the guy I play soccer with.'

'Pete,' the man says.

Joe shakes the big hairy hand; the man's grip is surprisingly gentle.

'I haven't been to Lakes Entrance since I was a kid,' Joe offers. He wishes he had a guidebook so he would know his place here.

Pete grunts. 'Won't have changed.'

'Do you fish?'

'Of a weekend.'

'My dad used to take me fishing. St Kilda pier.'

Deck rolls his eyes. 'I'd rather cut off my own ear than go fishing. So fucking boring.'

Pete smiles. 'It's what you make of it.'

Joe is surprised at the man's patience. Maybe the swagger is more assurance than aggression.

He thinks of his own diminutive family. It's been months since he called his mother. She leaves messages on his phone and sometimes he texts her. He knows he should see her but he can't stomach her helpless concern: if she could just not look at him that way. He hasn't spoken to his dad in a few years—he has a new family up north. But he does remember the fishing. It was probably only a handful of Sundays but the memories have acquired an enduring, sitcom quality, they've been aired so many times.

Riding on the back of his dad's Honda, visor down on his little red helmet, out along Beaconsfield Parade. Burying his hands into the pockets of his dad's slippery leather jacket in the fear he'd slide off the back without anyone noticing. Then some footage is missing—they must have parked and gone to the kiosk for bait—until, here they are, dangling their feet off the end of the pier. Handlines with lead sinkers and single hooks, smelly bits of chopped-up squid, his dad's rusty hunting knife. It was basic. But on at least one of those occasions they caught a couple of flathead. He recalls standing at a running tap, watching the knife slice through the slimy brown skin, his dad's big fingers scooping out the guts then carefully separating the heart to show Joe. He is looking down at his own small bare feet beside the fish's heart still visibly pumping. His dad is laughing. A tiny liver-coloured organ, separated from its host, moving sideways on the wet concrete, still animate; fighting for life, beyond reason or even choice.

It was his first taste of death: he thought it was something you could master.

Marie lights the candles and they sing; Granny leads in a tremulous soprano. The stepdad doesn't come in but watches through the window, phone to his ear, deadpan. Deck hiding behind his shawl of hair, cracking a reluctant smile when Joe winks. They eat wedges of cake and cream.

The next-door neighbours arrive—a middle-aged couple. They are Deck's 'uncle' and 'aunt', with a wrapped present and a slab of beer. Marie has turned on the Stones. There will be a good time had here tonight.

Deck and Joe go outside and kick a ball for a while but the sun is falling fast and Joe has to drop the car back and get to work.

'Thanks for coming and that,' Deck says to him, unbidden.

'Thanks for asking me.'

'Fuck off then.'

'Be good.'

He takes a circuitous route home after the bar closes so he can tic tac up the narrow space created by two new apartment buildings on High Street; a corridor he discovered last week, designed for wheelie bins. Climbs high—vertical steps—sweet momentum—up one storey, two—to rest on someone's window ledge, legs dangling. Their blind is drawn against the chill but he can hear a television turned up loud to compete with the radio from another room. Combined, they create a soundtrack of jangled suspense. He is silent as a cat. What it is to be up here, looking down; to sense the drop and the pull of it.

It's not long before dawn when he footbrakes beside the laundromat and turns in. The house is dark, but as soon as he steps inside he feels her. Pauses in the corridor like a thief.

'Hi.' Her voice—tentative and disembodied.

She's in the living room. The light is off but the TV is casting eerie coloured patterns across the mournful woollen hyacinth.

He perches on the arm of the couch and looks at the screen, talks out of the side of his mouth. 'Winding down after work?'

'Yeah. Shift from hell. Two motorbike accidents. Severe head injuries. I lost one of them. The other won't walk again.'

He turns to her in the quavering light. 'That would be hard.'

'It's harder with the ones you've seen out yourself, but it's the truth, isn't it? We all die. When we're washing down the body with warm water, zipping it into the canvas bag, heave-hoeing it onto the green trolley, we always wish them well on their final camping trip.'

He nods slowly, can't take his eyes off of her. 'Yeah, it's the truth.'

'Sometimes I think I'm lucky: ICU is like the holding zone between life and death. Everything matters, every detail.'

'I visited someone in ICU once,' Joe says. 'I remember the machines and alarms and little flashing lights. And the smell—it was like a science lab.'

'You get used to it. It was my plan B—nursing. Plan A didn't work out.'

'You're saving for a trip.'

'Yeah, working nights is good. I'm saving heaps.'

'I'm saving too. I'm not sure what for.' He has been putting money away for almost two years—not a lot but he spends little, and the egg has quietly grown. It sits there in his account, posing whitely for some unknown thing that's going to present.

'Maybe you'll know what it's for when you've saved enough?'

He hesitates, but in this moment he feels he could ask her anything. 'What if you don't? Know, I mean. When enough is enough.'

'Are we still talking about savings?'

'Money. Booze. Drugs. Or making good, say. Making amends.'

'You'll know, Joe.' In this light, she is incandescent. 'You just will.'

He is twisting towards her, balanced on the arm of the couch, his lithe, trustworthy body teetering on this precipice.

Searching one another's eyes—it's like staring into the abyss. 'I like your pyjamas,' he says quietly. 'Cute.'

'I was hoping you would come home. I was sort of waiting.'

'You were?'

'Yeah, I was.'

'For me.'

'For you.'

'I'm confused.'

'You're not confused.'

She reaches up. She takes his hand. The first touch of her cool skin is exquisite. Just as he knew it would be; just as he imagined. And without moving a muscle he starts to relinquish. He knows it. She does too. Sweeping down her body with his eyes, scooping up the whole breathtaking spotted-flannel length of her. When he returns to her eyes they are blurry and full of want. He has lost his rudder.

'I don't know if this is such a good idea.' He gestures towards the corridor, the house. 'Could make things complicated.'

'Only if we let it.'

'And I'm out of practice.' Half-smiling, but his eyes implore her. 'I haven't done this in a while.'

'Do you want to do this?' She implores him back.

He frowns. 'You know that I do.'

The TV flickers and time stop-starts-stop-starts as he runs his fingers slowly up her arm to her neck, light across her breastbone. She shudders: he can feel it under his hand. Then he is moving his body down to the couch in a neat curve, like he is under the bridge, playing. Kissing her. And she is kissing him back. After all the weeks of yearning it is urgent; pushing hard up against one another; mouths, hands. She strokes his cock through his jeans. 'Yeah, you want to do this.'

He pulls back to look at her, unbuttoning her pyjama top so he can see that it is happening, that it is real—thumbs rubbing over her hard nipples. Leaning in again with his mouth. Pulling off the rest of her pyjamas. She is so perfect. She is like fucking ice-cream.

He helps her drag down his jeans and she climbs over him, entwining her fingers through his and holding tight, like they are going on a scary ride. Her soft cool body tight over his; pushing up into her, faster and harder. It is like leaping over rooftops, fucking like this, he had forgotten. The bottomless hunger. The happiness. Straight to the terrible heart of it. 'Don't stop,' he moans. Suddenly as afraid as he is excited.

She is breathless in his ear. 'I am right here.'

Time, later, to regret.

Entangled with her on the couch, spent, he can smell the musty carpet, hear the low canned laughter from the TV. She caresses his palms. He hasn't been touched like this for such a long time. 'Your hands are like leather. Like you've been working down the mines. What the hell have you been doing?'

'When I go running, sometimes I climb things. And jump. Sometimes I hit the ground hard.'

Her sleepy eyes light up. 'Can I come? I want to climb things with you.'

'I'm damaged goods.' He runs his finger down the neat track of her spine. 'I can't keep you safe.'

She stretches out, cat full of cream. 'You're not damaged goods, Joe. You're not even out of practice.'

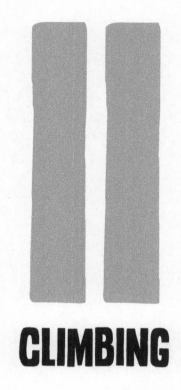

CLIMBING

6

'Go see your mother; it's been too long,' Joe's uncle Todd decrees, in his ashy bass-tone.

'It's true, Joey.' Sanjay adds this profound insight. He has come to help because he wants to avoid an essay. 'When did you last go home to the source?'

'Christmas.'

'So.' Todd is sitting in a foldout canvas chair, dappled in chlorophyll-green, furry eyebrows raised smugly.

'So. What.'

Every now and then Joe puts in a few hours at his uncle's nursery—potting, pruning, sweeping, lugging thirty-kilo bags of shit. His squat hairy uncle, who resembles a century-old fern, has rheumatoid arthritis that is slowly making knotted roots of his hands and his livelihood. He pays Joe for his time in homegrown weed and unsolicited advice.

'I'll say no more,' his uncle says.

'Good.'

They have potted upwards of eighty broccoli seedlings and a hundred-odd tiny leek into recycled pots. His uncle will sell these bouncy organic specimens alongside the limper commercial stock for the same price. It's why his business is still ticking over.

Joe crowds the seedlings into shallow plastic crates and Sanjay carries each crate to the corner signposted VEG, arranging them in a pleasing fashion on tree stumps. The winter sun overseeing the nursery yard is the kind that provides little warmth but plenty of probing light.

'Smoko?' Sanjay suggests.

They go into the kitchen-office, in earshot of the bell on the counter. Joe makes the coffee, because he can.

'And what about your plans,' Todd says, 'for the future.' It's more statement than question, as if it's his duty to remind Joe he should have some. This is how Deck must feel when Joe asks him about school. They are like a nest of Russian man-dolls.

'What happened to saying no more?'

'What, I can't speak at all?' Todd backs out to greet a customer, gnarly hands raised in a show of incredulity.

'Saved by the bell,' Joe mutters to Sanjay.

His plan, once, was to be a sports teacher. He always loved games—any game, he was undiscerning. In primary school his life's goal was to play soccer professionally. Still has a dog-eared poster of Maradona in full flight pinned to the inside of his wardrobe door. If the soccer didn't work out, maybe he could be a tennis diva. He could sweat and swear. He had exquisite self-control—even at ten. He was good at most of it because no matter the sport, it was all gut and muscle and flow. It was where he lost and found himself. On a cricket pitch or soccer field or basketball court he would know exactly where everyone was and what they were doing—and about to do—without any conscious effort. Later, he would think a good game was not all that different from good sex.

Then the morbidity of adolescence: he stopped training, took his eye off the ball, lost his proprioception. He misplaced his own body and that intuitive sense of how it interacted with the world. His dad left, too, and so he got up to lots of no good. *You only have one brain, don't chew it up*, his uncle would warn, but this was just provocation. He was desperate to prove he had nothing to prove. He could be a big man without anyone to show him how. It became more important to bend the rules than his legs; to take what wasn't his; to get high and hook up and drop out.

But then Jen came and things mattered again. Everything mattered. By the end of their final year he had decided he would be a sports teacher, applying to do a Bachelor of Applied Science in phys ed at RMIT. He liked being around kids. He liked their springiness and wide eyes. As a teacher he would get to keep playing and he and Jen could take long summer holidays by the sea. She was going to be a scientist and discover something huge. They would have the four kids.

'Planning is overrated,' Joe tells his uncle when he returns from serving a customer.

'So is free and easy,' Todd hits back.

'You call this free and easy?' Joe holds up his dirty hands.

And then Sanjay comes to his defence. 'Don't worry, Uncle. Our friend Joe is on a sacred journey.' With great earnestness: 'He is going to surprise us.'

'Boo,' Joe says, deadpan.

He clenches and unclenches his fists, strengthening the flexors, opponens and abductors in his hands, wrists and forearms, the muscles he needs for good grip. He has an urge to hit something, but these days he can see past these urges—into a panorama of pointlessness.

They finish their coffee in a silence marred only by the noisy miners. Joe notices his uncle using both hands to pick up his cup; Todd notices Joe noticing. Joe winces at him in sympathy and Todd puts down his cup and reaches over to touch his nephew's face.

Then, 'Well, if you want the nursery, you two can have it,' as a casual aside.

Joe laughs. With his worsening disability, his uncle has a newfound impatience but also a sweet largesse, sending Joe home after these working bees with woollen jumpers or favourite books. An old brass knife and scabbard. A tablecloth embroidered by his great-grandmother. Things that Joe puts in a cardboard box on top of his wardrobe.

'I don't have the money or the talent.' Joe gestures to the seedlings. 'They don't like the sound of my voice.'

But Sanjay is looking around, head tilted to one side, appraising. Joe kicks his shin.

Todd shrugs. 'I can't keep it up much longer. I'm dead serious. Sanjay, you're a hortie, and Joe—you could do anything you set your mind to. At least think about it.'

Joe murmurs his assent, and gets up to wash their mugs. The least he can do for his uncle. After all Todd has done for him.

The three men head back out to the nursery and pot up a few dozen broad beans, then Todd gives Sanjay the gear to roll a takeaway joint, joints being too fiddly for Todd's hands. Joe's reward is an old Bob Dylan t-shirt, neatly folded in a plastic bag hanging from the branch of a small crepe myrtle.

Todd sees them out, patting their heads.

Sanjay smokes the joint as they walk home, cackling every time Joe jumps onto a fence, clambers up a wall. 'I love your funny tricks, Joey. I tell you, they make me happy as a lark.'

The tiny terrace gallery in Collingwood is packed. He can't get close to the etchings on the walls, can't see Lena; takes a mineral water from a passing tray, then a dumpling; rocks back and forth on his feet, imagines he is on a rail, finds his balance. He is not quite sure why he has come. He will give it fifteen minutes then split.

Eventually she appears from a room out back, carrying a tray of food. Of course.

When she finally makes her way over to him, she reaches up to kiss his cheek. The kiss is new, but so is the context. And they are friends, right? You can be friends with a girl.

'Should have known you'd be working.'

She rolls her eyes. 'Yeah, we go way back, me and Nadja. We went to school together. What do you think? Do you like the little worlds?'

'Is that what they are?'

She puts the tray down on a side table and takes his hand, pulls him towards the nearest wall. He notices that the feel of her hand is okay, even nice—her chef's palms are tough like his. She could be a teammate, a sister. He doesn't draw back; and then she lets him go.

They have to get right up close. The copper etchings are no bigger than envelopes but they hold exquisitely intricate cityscapes. Unidentifiable landmarks stand silent witness to complex social interactions. 'I like the dogs,' Lena says.

He looks for the dogs. Some are unattended, wandering loose; others carried under arms or on leashes. Some are wearing hats. In one etching, a gang of dogs is terrorising a woman and her child.

'My dad breeds German shepherds,' he tells her. Last heard, that is.

'Ugh. They conjure secret police.'

'Do they?'

'Yes.' Her eyes twinkle.

They walk the perimeters of both small rooms and eat more pan-Asian tidbits. He should have brought Sanjay; he loves all this shit. 'So you went to school together.'

'Uh-huh. She's Ukrainian. Our families were close—cocktail parties and Christmas and stuff.'

Lena pauses to get a glass of mulled wine and is knocked from behind, spilling it down his t-shirt. 'Shit! Sorry.' She gets a handful of napkins and dabs at him.

'It's fine. Just like being at work.' The t-shirt is navy blue—the stain won't show. He refills her glass from the crockpot on the drinks table. 'Too much cinnamon,' he comments, sniffing.

'You think? It's my recipe. Try it.'

So he does, he takes a sip. Nothing bad happens; he hands it back. 'Not too sweet—I like that. Yeah, go easy on the cinnamon next time.'

They head outside for a cigarette. 'So I made up your back story,' she tells him, as they lean against the glass of the tailor next door.

'Oh yeah.'

'So. The carp. He was your grandfather. He came from a muddy freshwater river in Sicily where he grew fat on the flesh of drowned mobsters. I am sure you have some Italian blood in you.'

'Irish.'

'Fine. It was a river winding through a mossy green valley. Your grandmother was a strong woman, very special, but she was cast out of her village when she married the fish. They were forced to migrate and start a new life.'

'It's always exile with you,' he teases. 'Everyone is in exile.'

'You are telling me you are not familiar with this feeling? I don't believe you. Exile is a state. It can be self-imposed or imposed by others.'

He sighs and pulls on his cigarette. 'Go on.'

'Your father, half fish, is slippery. You don't trust him. And he breeds standover dogs.'

'He did used to take me fishing.'

'You see!'

'He's too dull to be slippery.' He takes another sip of her drink.

'He is matt not gloss?'

'Exactly.'

'Okay. Perhaps your mother is half fish?'

'No, my mother is an owl.'

'Wise?'

'Watchful. She doesn't like to join in. I don't know if she's wise. I'm too stupid to tell.'

Lena snickers.

'What?' He can't help smiling back at her.

'My ploy has worked. I have begun to extract your history.'

He shoves her sideways and she laughs. He thinks that she would be hard to break; he likes that. He is tempted to shove her again but contains himself.

They finish smoking in an easy quiet. 'I'm going back in to help.'

'Cool. I'm heading home. I'll see you.'

'Yes, and I will see you.'

He doesn't say, *I am heading home to fuck the nurse*—he never knows, anyway, when the nurse will appear. She slips in and out of the house like a wisp of smoke; he can't track her.

After walking a couple of blocks he breaks into a gentle run. The sense of anticipation is strong but he is in no hurry. He goes the back way, meets up with his favourite course at the laneway, where he mounts the wall and travels cat balance along its crest. In the murky playground, partially lit by a streetlamp, he moves backwards and forwards on the bars, three at a time, using his whole body to swing like a gibbon. Then he does a dead hang for five aching minutes, pulling his shoulders back to protect the sockets, his earthly body dragging him down. He can smell the orange and spice of his t-shirt, allowing himself the uncomplicated pleasure of recalling the gallery: the etchings and human hum; the safe harbour of Lena, laughing, lips stained mahogany with the mulled wine.

The dead hang is nice conditioning for grip and upper-body endurance; vital for climbing and *lache,* underbars and cat leaps. It stretches out the torso and decompresses the spine. He drops.

As he approaches the laundromat he hears music and rounds the corner to look in. Someone has set up an amp inside the lit interior and a guy is playing Van Morrison on his electric guitar. A dozen or so others sit around in friendly communion on the tall white sorting tables, nodding heads, drinking beers. Someone beckons to Joe to enter but he smiles and backtracks, vaults over the closed gate.

There is a low glow emanating from the lean-to: a beacon. He slips his key into the lock.

On Sunday morning Elise is working at the kitchen table; Adam has retreated to his study upstairs. She's doing a small job for a local council, branding a free exercise program they've introduced to make it look like they're doing something to tackle obesity. The flier is about done; she's just playing with background colours. Nothing really redeems the council's school-uniform-purple logo.

The kitchen smells like coffee and bacon—really, *she* should be doing more bloody exercise, a swim every week or two is hardly cutting it. The sun at the window is all sparkly lemon, a visual accompaniment to the warmth of the oil heater. Carl has said he will drop by in the afternoon so she is counting down the hours. Maybe she could convince him to stay for dinner.

Something changes in the room. She looks up to see Adam standing in the doorway, watching her. They don't really look at each other anymore, so when she smiles it is unguarded.

'I'm leaving.'

'Where are you going? Carl's coming over later.'

'Lise, I am leaving.'

She is bewildered—frowning while enjoying the rare candour in his eyes, a tenderness in his voice. 'I don't understand.'

He clears his throat. 'I've been sitting up there trying to work out what to say, but I couldn't. I couldn't write the summation. So I've got nothing. I'm sorry. The thing is, there *is* nothing to say.' He is gesturing vaguely with his elegant hand, from her to him, her to him.

'Oh.' The sense of unreality—the high gloss of shock—that settles into their cosy kitchen is stunningly familiar. Or is this in fact reality that's come knocking again, and what's the difference? 'So you've just decided to call it a day?'

He closes his eyes and rubs his fingers up and down the bridge of his nose. 'Listen to your schoolmarm voice. Please. You cannot be surprised.'

'How would you know how I feel?'

'I don't exist for you anymore. You don't even see me.'

'That is ridiculous. You walk into this house and barely register my presence. I'd have to commit a felony to get your undivided attention.'

'That's not true. It's not true at all. But we are obviously feeling the same way.'

'And you're probably having an affair. Are you?'

'No.' He looks at her, clears his throat again.

'But?'

'I was propositioned. Nothing happened.'

She laughs. 'You were *propositioned*? And so now you want to do things properly and leave first, because you want to be the good guy.'

'Yes. I want to do things properly. Is that wrong?'

'You're not the good guy, Adam. You're a walking fucking zombie.'

With no communication between her brain and her body she is standing and sweeping the laptop, water glass, phone, papers and crayons off the table. The clatter as inanimate objects bump off chairs and onto the floor is good, but it is not enough.

She walks to the window that looks out onto the winter garden of their family home. Pulls back her right arm and smashes her fist through that clear, hard barrier with every fibre of strength left in her.

Exquisite relief. Blood drip-drip-drips to the floor. The heart of the house has finally stopped beating.

Adam gets tea towels and wraps them loosely over her hand, wanting to staunch the bleeding without further embedding the glass. She lets him do it—amazing, the calm. And she speaks gently, as if his wound is the more pressing, in need of suppuration. 'You want to walk out so you can go and fuck the new partner. It's okay, Adam. I understand. Go. Get out of here.'

He shakes his head. 'It's not like that, Lise.'

'When you speak to her you laugh. You take the phone to your study. It all starts to make sense.' Her hand is only now beginning to hurt. 'I think I might hate you.'

'I know you do.'

'My heart is broken.'

'So is mine.'

She nods. Retrieves her phone from the floor and navigates the screen with her left hand. 'I'm going to ask Jill to take me to the doctor,' she explains.

'Let me.'

'No.' She is already walking away.

7

Early hours: the soft turn of a key; almost indiscernible click of the lock re-engaging. Knows it's the nurse: she has those rubber shoes and treads so lightly the dodgy floorboards don't creak. He pictures her padding down long hospital corridors, turning those interminable corners with the little grey signs and arrows, yellow stethoscope swinging towards life, now death. Life? Death?

She knocks gently.

'Yeah.'

Steps through; sits on the edge of his bed. 'I knew you'd be awake.' Impish: 'Wanna run?'

'Now?'

She has closed the door and they are whispering. 'Well, yeah.'

'Where are your scrubs?'

'Ditched them. I looked like a butcher.'

'Hard night?'

'Yeah, it got a bit messy. Had this guy presenting with asthma but he didn't respond to the mask or intubation. So finally we got these two big pipettes into his thighs and drained all the blood out of his body. Oxygenated it and chucked it back in. Up go his SATs, right as rain.'

'A good news story. Nice. Okay, I'll come. Give me a minute.'

She doesn't move; just sits there watching him. So he holds her eyes as he climbs out of bed naked, pulls on pants, a sweatshirt. She whistles; he laughs.

'I want you to show me your favourite route.'

He jogs backwards, watching her. In a grey tracksuit and bouncy little black runners, black sweatband around her head. Sweet. 'Tell me when you've had enough,' he says, pulling away.

Sunrise is still a way off but his eyes rapidly adjust to the dark. He's always liked running at night. Streetlamps cast misshapen circles of light onto the tarmac so that their figures appear and disappear, on and off, like stagehands.

He goes slow at first, thinking she will struggle to keep up, but she is right there at his side. So he speeds up and vaults over the rail; she follows. It's clumsy—she comes down too hard and twists a little—but still.

They stamp fresh tracks across the grass with its fine tinsel of dew, and then spend some time warming up in the playground: squats, lunges, pull-ups.

'Joe, can we do something fun now? You know, jumping across roofs or something?'

'You need to start at ground level.'

''Kay, Grandad.'

He shakes his head and tsks at her. This is a new role. 'Parkour isn't about being reckless. It's about focus and training and understanding your own limits. With every new move you have to break it down and work on each part before putting it back together. Otherwise you are going to hurt yourself.'

She nods gravely. 'And you'll teach me?'

'I taught myself. I'm no expert. I can show you some stuff.'

They start with a low drop and roll off a platform attached to the fort, roughly five feet high. He demonstrates how the key to safe landing is in redistributing the shock throughout the body, so that it dilutes along chains of muscles rather than impacting one or two. 'And obviously you never roll over your head or along your spine.'

'Obviously.'

She practises dropping onto the spongy plum play surface—
'Ouch,' she says, laughing, every time she hits the ground. But
they keep at it until she is rolling smoothly on the diagonal,
from the left shoulder across the back to the opposite hip,
buttock, thigh. Rising up into a run.

'You're good,' he tells her. 'You're fast.'

'Better late than never.'

They run back to the house via the 7-Eleven, where he
buys bread; creep down the corridor to his bed. Shed clothes.
She nestles into his arms, back to front, and they watch the
world slowly come to light through his window. He can feel
his heartbeat slow and loud against her still form.

'I don't think we should tell anyone about this,' she says.
'It'll be awkward for the others. And, you know, I'm going
soon—we don't have long.'

'Okay. Sure. Let's cancel the skywriter.'

'It'll be more fun anyway—our secret.'

And it is fun: it's like a beautiful dream. She rolls over
and they kiss for ages, for the hell of it, like teenagers, kissing
with intent. Then Joe goes to the kitchen and comes back with
coffee and peanut butter sandwiches.

She isn't hungry so he eats hers too. 'Too much gore last
night—stole my appetite.'

He shows her his favourite YouTube clip, of the Tokyo cat leap. And they talk about anatomy and physiology—the nurse quotes from *Mosby's*—but also the mind as the key muscle that has to be trained to overcome.

'The spirit leads,' she murmurs. Weary now. 'The body follows.'

'Amen.' He strokes her scruffy head.

Before the sun has risen above the houses she glides down the corridor and into the lean-to, to her mask and earplugs, to block out the day that she may sleep.

———

Elise goes to stay for a spell at Jill's art deco apartment in St Kilda overlooking the water. She can't yet face the house.

'This could be me.' Besocked feet up on the coffee table, looking out at the choppy grey bay, rain threatening. She has been sleeping on the three-seater suede couch, her bag of clothes and toiletries—thrown together after their bloody visit to Emergency—tucked neatly under the coffee table. 'Maybe I could find somewhere like this and we could be neighbours.'

Jill has her feet up too, sprawled on the armchair opposite, nursing a mug of tea. She has a soft, pensive expression by default and often looks mildly surprised—something to do with her neat little eyebrows. 'That sounds superb, but I don't think so.'

'Why not?'

'Adam will be back. And you'll take him.'

'Pah. Two unlikelihoods. He's probably going to move in with the young partner and start a new family. They'll have beady-eyed lawyer babies.'

Jill's tricoloured cat Pip is clawing Elise's leg. 'Pip' because Jill rescued him from a back alley and gave him great expectations. Elise pulls his talons out of her jeans using her good hand and strokes his sleek coat. All that fancy food in foil and cardboard packets, Pip need never hunt again.

Saturday afternoon, and they have been reading newspapers on their iPads. Hardly newspapers if they don't leave ink on your fingertips. Eating crackers and cheese and sliced apples. They even listened to a radio play.

'*Would* you take him back?'

'I don't think so. He's right that there's nothing left. We just remind one another every day of what we've lost.'

'It wasn't always the way, though. There was lots of other stuff you shared.'

'Yeah, but you can't go back, can you. Nothing can ever be undone.'

They slide into silence. Elise plays Scrabble on her tablet;

occasionally Jill reads out a passage from one of the Year 11 essays she is correcting, the outrage and optimism of youth skipping hand in hand. The two women first met in those capricious days—first-year uni, both from the country and living on campus, learning how to fend for themselves.

The room gradually dims.

'Let me buy you dinner,' Elise offers. 'I've done nothing all week.' Her right arm is still in a sling to remind her not to use it.

So Jill lends her a scarf and they walk together up the road, past all the young things in their Saturday-night best. Elise doesn't quite trust how easy all this is, and yet she isn't numb exactly. Her hand throbs a little—it does that at the end of the day—and when she peers ahead, into the coming days, weeks, years, she feels like she is falling. But here now, with her closest friend, first stars are appearing from behind the thick curtain of clouds.

They arrive at the pub and find a table by the wall, order stout and stodgy dinners.

'Anyway, you're the one who's been having the affair,' Jill points out.

'Ha. If you could call it that.'

'I think you could. Secret rendezvous. Passion. Deception. Guilt.'

'They're tigers.' Elise came clean with Jill at the hospital last week—something about her relief at being wounded, her need to see blood. She had to try to explain.

'Remember how she was going to get the tattoo?' Jill asks.

Elise smiles. 'Silly girl.'

'Are you going to show me your drawings?'

'Not yet. I will. Soon. I promise.'

They eat, and down the dark beer. She goes to the bar and gets two more. She could live like this: without fresh greens and home-baked bread and all other futile attempts at goodness.

'Hey, I'm thinking about long-service leave,' Jill says. 'It's coming up . . . start of next year.'

'That sounds excellent. You're burnt out, aren't you? You need a long break from those pesky kids.'

'Yeah, just a bit.'

'What will you do? Write that Aztec novel at last?'

'I want to take a trip. I haven't done that in over ten years. I don't know where—but something a bit epic.'

'A bit epic. And you're the English teacher.'

They drink and talk about bucket lists, then wander back towards the apartment, hitting the shore this time. It has started to softly rain but the stars are still twinkling and the sea invites, so halfway along they perch on the wall to yank off their shoes. And to hell with fudgy condoms and contaminated needles.

———

It's 3.45 on Sunday afternoon when he turns into the street where he grew up. Caught a bus partway and ran the rest. He has to be at the bar at five, which gives them all of thirty minutes. He has 'suggested topics of conversation' in his head, and he blagged another bag of crescent biscuits from the cafe so that he has something tangible to give her. He will act like they saw each other last week.

The reticent suburban street is curved like a smile with weatherboard teeth. He sees that Carmelo has finally built his brick shed, for tinkering, and the Gilberts have a new letterbox shaped like a hotdog. The milk bar at the eastern end of the street, where he used to buy bread and cigarettes with Jen, now sells bric-a-brac. It looks dusty and pointless; it's not like there's any foot traffic. But she would have liked it, he thinks. Can picture her walking alongside him on the footpath, twirling a string bag, trying to lure him into the shop with the promise of treasure. To which he would have said, *As if.*

A few houses short of the Californian bungalow that once belonged to his grandparents—bestowed on his mother, the child in greatest need—he hesitates. A new neighbour, a man he doesn't recognise, is mowing his front lawn; two boys play on skateboards in the driveway, scooting to the top of the slight incline before fizzing down.

Closes his eyes and breathes, then opens them, holding the paper sack of biscuits aloft, does a running jump clear over his mother's woven-wire fence, landing soft on the balls of his feet. Walks calmly up the path to her front door.

She's never been affectionate, his mother, and when she opens the door he is greeted by her peculiarly flat expression, as if she is waiting for him to announce himself.

He laughs. 'Aren't you expecting me? The text this morning?'

A veil lifts, and she pulls him into an awkward embrace. She is a whole head shorter than him and somehow doesn't feel like a mother should. He pats her small birdlike back and she sighs, almost a shudder. 'It's okay,' he says to her automatically.

They go inside, and to the kitchen. She has laid out the custard-coloured teacups and saucers, matching jug of milk, on the round wooden table. Everything is as it was. Talking radio turned down low, slatted blinds angled steep north so light can get in but nothing else.

Jen loved these teacups. She didn't find this room claustrophobic—she found it cosy.

'Let me put the kettle on,' his mother says.

Here, he will drink tea; here, tea serves a purpose.

He puts the biscuits on the table. 'Mum, the house needs paint.'

'Yes. I know.'

They pull out chairs and sit down opposite one another. He stares at the grain of the table, strokes his hand across it. The cool smoothness conjures the nurse's body and he feels a wash of desire—of all the inappropriate things.

'You look well,' he says, meeting her gaze. Steady.

'I'm fine.' She peers at him out of her large nocturnal eyes. 'What about you, darling?'

'Good. Busy.'

They talk for fifteen minutes or so about matters of little interest. Changes in the neighbourhood. Her work. His. The weather.

Then, 'Todd says you've been coming in. He's very grateful.'

'His hands are getting bad.'

'He thinks of you like a son.' She gets up to refill the teapot. 'Did you know that?'

Joe shrugs.

'He wants you to be happy.'

He leans over the back of the chair, letting his body relax into the stretch, gravity pulling him down through his arms. Exhales as he straightens. 'Can we just not?'

'Not *what*, Joe?'

'Start on my happiness.'

'How long will you go on punishing yourself?'

He smiles crookedly. 'Mum, this is why I don't come to see you.'

'It's because I love you, Joe. She loved you too! It's been over three years.'

'I know how long it has been. I can even tell the time.'

'You can't keep running.'

He groans. His hands are fists under the table. There is much he will endure, but not this. 'This is not fucking *Home and Away*. You are not helping.'

They sit in silence for eternity.

'Okay,' she says. 'Let me just say this one thing. You need to forgive yourself.'

He stands up, can't help laughing. She can't see how it's funny. He is running late for work now: perfect.

'I'm sorry,' she says at the door. 'I know I say the wrong thing.'

He doesn't disagree. But punishing her is not like punishing himself. 'Do you want me to paint the house?' He rips a blister of paint off the doorframe. 'It looks shit.'

And of course she is delighted.

This he can do for her.

8

They sneak around. And go out to play—running, climbing, jumping. She is a fast learner: she is preternatural.

He introduces her to the bridge; his secret. They run there before dawn one midweek day and he breaks the implicit parkour code: showing off for her shamelessly. She claps her hands with glee as he climbs up onto the railway tracks and does a kong vault over the handrail, sailing ten feet, landing neatly on the gravel below. A move he mastered six months ago, after six months of focused work and countless failed attempts.

Then they head back down to the northern underside and he wets the soles of his Feiyue with saliva, does some wall runs up the brick pillar. Because she is there, looking on, he makes it all the way to those six bolts some twelve feet high. 'Is he a man or is he a fucking spider?' she says, laughing.

It's harder to see down here under the bridge, in the dark. There is just illumination enough from nearby streetlights, from a half-moon. She does basic balance work on the wedge of embedded rail while he precision-jumps back and forth from the rail to the low concrete wall. Then she scales the dedicated climbing wall with the concrete blobs for grip. Up down sideways. Her arms tire quickly. Patience, he says. Practice. Endless repetition. He describes the day early on that he came here and did two hundred climb-ups, how he could barely use his arms for a week.

Pulls her up by the hand onto the concrete platform tucked beneath the end of the rail bridge. Rolls a cigarette. She doesn't smoke—or eat, it would seem. He has slipped his hand under her hoodie; rests it on her breastbone. She is so thin. 'After your trip to the top of the mountain, or wherever it is you are going, what then?' He is thinking of himself.

'No plans.'

'Will you come back?'

She rests her head in his lap so she can look up into his eyes. 'I am hoping new opportunities will arise, abroad, wherever. I'm kind of seeing it as a permanent thing.'

He shakes his head. 'You came out of nowhere.'

Tell me, he wants to say. *Where have you* been? But they have agreed not to talk of the past, knowing they have no future. It's why he can't get enough of her. It's why he lets himself have her at all.

They will be in the living room watching TV and he will glance up and find her looking at him in that sardonic way. He'll turn deliberately back to the screen. Ignore her. Then as soon as Sanjay and Jack have gone to bed he'll creep down to her room and they'll make love silently, on her mattress on the floor, hands laced over one another's mouths.

It seems incredible no one can see what is happening.

'You didn't come out of nowhere though, did you, Joe?' she says, smiling, under the bridge.

He laughs. 'Are you calling me slow?'

'No. I'm saying I found you just where you were meant to be.'

Friday night at the bar is a whiteout. Joe spins in and out of the kitchen, broad back first through the swinging doors. Every contender in the inner north has turned up to play, so they get behind on orders. The bar girls are giving away freebies to impatient customers. Boss gets mad at everyone. Lena fires back that they're chronically fucking understaffed and he's lucky she doesn't call the fucking union. Waving a machete around. Boss retreats, swearing in Greek. Through this and the night's other balancing acts and spillages—plates along each of Joe's arms like a circus act; the customer banter and tips—he and Lena keep up a constant raillery that serves as a guide rope leading them blindly on.

Show over, doors closed, they stand together in the kitchen eating leftovers with their hands.

'They got a happy ending, though, your grandparents,' he says, continuing some long-ago conversation. They do this.

'Yes. But they were made crazy by their lives. They survived the Holodomor—Stalin's forced famine. Why do you think I cook for a living? Seriously, once my grandmother wept because I was on some stupid teenage diet. She said she wouldn't eat until I did.'

'So what happened? Did you kill your grandmother?'

'I learnt to lead a double life.'

Joe washes oil off his hands and takes the tips out of his apron pocket, counts the money out, divides it in half. They are good takings. 'Suckers,' he mutters.

'We earned every penny.'

'Service tonight was shit.'

'We still earned it.'

He stretches, rising up onto his forefeet, fingers touching the lip of the air vent.

'Whatcha doing now then, son of a carp?'

'Home.' Doesn't say that he wants to see the nurse; that he is gagging for it. 'You?'

'Might meet some friends for a drink. I need to wind down. I could have killed Boss tonight. He'll be lucky if I come back tomorrow.'

'I'll walk with you.'

They change and head out into the night. Lena is wearing her short leather jacket and a blue knitted beanie that matches her eyes. She looks carelessly sexy. But that would be a weird thing to note so he doesn't.

Then, apropos of nothing, as they are strolling along, 'Joe, are you getting laid?'

'Huh?'

'Well?'

He whistles. 'That's blunt, Lena. And so American.'

'I *knew* it. It's in your face. Who's the lucky girl then?'

He hesitates. Doesn't want this conversation. 'Just a girl.'

'Charming.'

'What do you want me to say? She's five foot seven.'

She seems to think on this long and hard, and he distracts himself with the streetlights, imagines climbing their trunks, *lache* along the power lines. 'Actually, I don't want you to say anything,' she concludes. 'I don't need the details. Glad you're having a good time.'

Silence ensues and he feels like he's been caught with his pockets full of stolen sweets, like the time in Year 7 when his mother made him take the loot back to the milk bar. She was right—it was more chocolate than he could possibly eat. He was banned from the shop for six months.

After another block, Lena drops her board and wishes him a good night. He wants to hold her up, to explain—but what? They are not lovers: they are friends. And, as if reading his mind, again, she gives him a lewd wink under the streetlight and punches his arm. Hits the pavement with her boot and rolls away.

House black as liquorice, empty as sugar. The nurse is not here. Fuck it. He switches on lights and wanders through the rooms, scanning the detritus, the textbooks and bills, damp towels and sunglasses. Leaves them where they are: he is not the fucking cleaner.

Goes to his room and sits on the edge of the bed. Thinks of the nurse and gets hard. It's difficult to conjure her face or fix her frame in his mind's eye, but he can see her soft white breasts, her dark nipples, and he puts his hands all over them.

Strokes his cock till he comes. So much for abstinence—it seems there is nothing he can deprive himself of.

Guilt comes like a fist out of nowhere. And that feeling of old, like his capacity to harm is bounded only by his own imagination.

He activates the iPad and navigates quickly in—no foreplay this time—to Jen's profile pic.

It was the start of Year 12, mid-February or thereabouts. Too early in the year to be stressed about SACs and the girls taking a break from trying to destroy one another, loving it up instead. There were a few of them at the beach; it was good—he and Jen spent so much time alone. A couple of the girls had brought food from home—none of them had any money—and Peanut had brought a beach ball, so there was an argument on the tram about gender roles and how next time they came the people with penises would provide the picnic. Stupid jokes about penis-butter. He remembers, when they arrived, how he pointed out to Jen where he fished with his father on those two or three or maybe five occasions. Would he have remembered, without this picture, that she was wearing the red dress? They played keepings-off in the water. Dug tunnels. Ate all the food then coughed up for ice-cream; he had half of Jen's—she was cutting back on dairy or something. It was a hallowed day. Perhaps all of her days were hallowed.

'It was a good day, wasn't it?' he murmurs to her smiling face. She is mute.

He scrolls through a few more photos, but impatiently this time. Looking for something that will really hurt. Pauses at the photo taken before their formal, some nine months after the day at the beach. He is in a borrowed blue suit and she is wearing her mother's apple-green halter-neck dress. Their arms are locked around one another's waists, about to set off. It was taken just weeks before. If they could have known then how every minute would count. Yes. This should do it. Yes, this hurts.

And then, while he is weltering in it, a message pops up in the bottom right corner of the screen. Emily Dickinson.

Joe?

A tremor ripples the muscles of his back. He looks at the type. And talks himself into reason.

Who is this?

You wouldn't remember me. It's been a long time.

What the fuck? He doesn't respond.

I knew Jen.

She had a lot of friends.

I was wondering how you are these days?

Who is this?

Nothing.

More nothing.

He clicks to Emily Dickinson's page, but it is blank. No profile pic. No posts or albums, and—surprise surprise—no other friends.

The would-be poet must be one of Jen's girlfriends who disassociated when things got ugly that first year after; someone with a touch of nostalgia who wants to maintain a safe distance. Good of them to go to all this effort. It leaves him a little uneasy but he'd already got what he needed tonight: nice clean knife through the heart.

He waits a few minutes more then logs out.

Once the door of his consulting room has clicked shut behind them, and they are seated in the ugly periwinkle swivels, face to face, her GP is typically blunt: 'Are you suicidal?'

'No.' She smiles—embarrassed—and holds up her bandaged hand. 'I think I could do better than this.'

'Good. So what happened?'

She gives it to him broadly while he gently lifts off the gauze and attends to her wounds. 'They did a nice job,' he notes, gently palpating the flesh around the mends, checking for remaining shards. 'You're healing well.'

He gets his snips and starts to tug out the stitches. 'Does that hurt?'

She winces and shakes her head.

'Elise, I've suggested antidepressants before and I've respected your choice to go it alone. I admire how you've coped. But I have some concerns about how you are going to manage this new loss.'

Sitting in the patient's chair still makes her feel about five. 'It was impulsive. I won't do it again. I'm going to be fine.'

'When did you last see your psychologist? Willow, isn't it?'

'Oh, I don't know, a year or two ago?'

'Could I recommend we make an appointment? I can write you up a new mental health plan and send it to her direct.'

She sighs. 'Look, thanks. She was very helpful. But I think I've had enough grief counselling.'

'There is no timetable for this, Elise.'

'I know.'

He frowns. Why doesn't he just go ahead and tsk? 'I'd like you to come back in a few weeks and let me know how you're doing. Okay?'

'Yep. Sure.' As. If.

They stand up. 'What about marriage counselling? Have you two talked about it?'

'Not yet.'

'Let me know if you'd like me to recommend someone.'

He's a fine and fortunate man, the doctor, who sees a cure for everything.

She pays the bill and heads out to the tram stop. The day is slate-grey and windblown. Is Adam looking out his twenty-third-storey window on William Street at this same desolate world? Or is he looking in towards his lover, and all those clean legal edges?

She will make her slow way back across town to the shelter of Jill's apartment; needs just a little more of that time outside time. The only thing missing in St Kilda are the tigers and heaven knows they aren't going anywhere.

En route she responds to a text from Carl. She hasn't told him about the separation, postponing visits twice now with dubious excuses. He never probes, doesn't question. No doubt he is relieved. They've all got so good at stepping around.

The open finding is a formality, the coroner told them, in a white corridor, in a rush. *Your daughter was involved in a tragic accident—I'm almost certain. You would be surprised how often this sort of thing happens. Best if you can all find a way to move on.*

It's not like she went missing: the open finding a poor cousin of that particular brand of horror. They had her broken body and an adequacy of accounts. There was nothing more at all to be done. So they followed doctor's orders and tried to lay her to rest, doing the circle dance, ever more nimble, around residue sticky as blood.

9

Sunday morning, he and Sanjay pick up Todd and his gear then head north up Sydney Road to collect Deck. As instructed, Deck's sporting a parka over his skinny jeans, looking snugly unimpressed. It's been raining all night with no sign of letting up; perfect weather for mushrooming, Todd insists.

They drive forty-five minutes up the Calder and turn off towards Macedon. Todd navigates them on and off a series of increasingly narrow roads until an unmade track delivers them deep into the belly of a state-owned pine plantation.

At the very end of the season, pickings will be scant but so will tour groups. For half the drive Todd has bemoaned the flurry of restaurants and wineries trampling these sacred grounds with their busloads of curious customers. Is the extra buck worth it? When we are all in the know, what will be left to savour? Sanjay tut-tutted sympathetically; Joe drove; Deck listened to his iPod.

They park, unload, stretch. Winter suits these woods. There is little undergrowth and the canopy creates a sense of enclosure, the dark solid trunks of the pines rising like sentinels from the carpet of brown needles. Wind whistles.

They huddle around Todd. He has brought a stack of empty two-litre ice-cream containers; hands them around with an assortment of paring knives. Deck immediately puts a knife to his thumb to test its edge; looks at Joe to test his reaction; Joe rolls his eyes, shakes his head.

Todd leads them away from the road and into the woods for several hundred metres until he's found his first sweet spot. Then a brief tutorial, where they get up close to a saffron milk cap—convex, pooled with rain. Todd cuts through its hollow stem to show how the blood-orange milk seeps out. 'These are my personal favourite. Butter, garlic, salt and pepper, splash of wine . . . put 'em with eggs, ham, pasta . . .'

And not too far away, a hamlet of slippery jacks—slimy shit-coloured caps with yellow spongy undersides, pored instead of gilled. 'You have to peel these before you cook 'em, then they are chewy, meaty goodness courtesy of Mother Nature.'

Todd tells them to look out too for circles of tiny grey ghosts or the pale mauve-coloured wood blewits.

'You're not going to kill us, are you, Uncle? Remember the chef in Sydney? He was in a commercial kitchen, right?'

'They were death caps, Sanjay. Nothing like these babies. Poor bloke thought they were straw mushrooms. Don't worry. I've been doing this since I was wee.'

Todd shows them how to make a clean cut through the base of the fungus to promote new growth. Then they scatter, tools in hand, through the woods.

It is a treasure hunt, trudging over the clumpy ground, and a race: wanting to get there first, get the most, win the prize. In a show of support, the rain desists, the wind drops, and the icy-pole air is punctuated by cries of delight as pay dirt is hit.

'I am in heaven, bro.' Sanjay bowls up to Joe with his container one-third full. 'Really. I am going to have an orgasm right here in this forest.'

'Save it for your rich fantasy life. There are young people present.'

Sanjay springs off.

An hour passes; more. Joe has not been so lucky, moving outwards in a slow spiral—ineffective beside Sanjay's capering dot-to-dot. Deck has moved just fifty metres or so from the starting point. Looks miserable. Keeps fiddling with his phone, probably texting the new girlfriend, *WTF???*

Joe smiles to himself. It was time to introduce Deck to some of his people. Only fair.

'Oh, *yeah*,' Sanjay hollers from a few hundred metres away. 'I've just found me some succulent sweethearts.'

Todd sidles up to Joe and empties his mushrooms into Joe's container. 'No need to take pity on me,' Joe says. 'I can handle failure.'

But Todd isn't listening. 'Damn it,' he mutters in his old-wood voice. Tries to splay his muddy trembling hands but his knobbly fingers won't unfurl. 'I'm winding up, Joe. Look at it. Seizing up like a power tool made in China. Can't fix it. Can only buy a new one.'

'You found more than me,' Joe says, holding up his container. 'Shouldn't complain, right?'

'You can complain all you like. It's shit.'

'Pain isn't the problem. The weed helps with that. It's how useless I'm getting.' He leans in confidentially: a pointless gesture considering how far they are from anyone else. 'I'm having trouble at home. Opening things, and using the bloody stove. Don't say anything to your mother.'

'I wouldn't dream of it. But can't you get things, physical aides or whatever?'

Todd still isn't listening. 'And my toes! I'm not far from a walking stick, Joe. Would you credit it?'

They walk back to the car together. Todd fumbles out his fold-up chair and slumps while Joe collects twigs and pinecones and handfuls of needles from the base of a tree to build a small smoky fire on the open ground. In Todd's banana box are matches, a blackened billy, a tin of tea; four litres of water. Joe puts it together. Always with the fucking tea.

It starts to rain again and by the time the tea is ready the others have come back. Joe offers around the soggy sandwiches made by Todd. Cheese and tomato roughly cut.

At first they huddle under a tree but the sky, bored now with their petty foraging, determines to drive them away. They pack up as the embers sizzle. Climb inside the car in wet jeans with their hot drinks, steaming up the windows, mingling with the car's stale sugar and spice.

'You know fungi are their own separate life form, closer to animals than plants?' Sanjay offers.

Deck glowers at Joe from the back seat like all this is his fault. The indignity. Joe reaches over to ruffle his hair. 'Don't be downhearted,' he teases. 'We'll come again next year! You're sure to have more luck.'

They drive back listening to the footy, naked rubber lady

bouncing generously, cosy inside the Citroen, inside the driving rain.

Joe's phone dings when they hit the outskirts of the city: text from his mother: *Have a look at Dulux Paperbark.*

'You see,' he says, showing Todd. 'I've been good.'

Todd smiles. 'That you have.'

In Coburg, Deck can barely summon a 'later'. Up the path and into the unit head down, hands stuffed in pockets. He declined his share of the day's yeasty spoils but Joe is still glad he brought him along.

—

Elise stays in St Kilda for three weeks.

Every night when Jill gets home from work, they walk along the beach in their overcoats. After, Elise brings Jill a mug of tea or glass of gin while she marks papers or prepares lessons, or together they watch TV. They eat baked beans on toast more than once. Go to the pub on a whim. It reminds her of college days when they first became friends; a visitation to a simpler time when they only looked forward—wifedom, motherhood, things dreamt of or scorned. There is a great relief in relinquishing it all for a bit. And bolts of grief: she's not twenty anymore. She is sleeping on a couch because her husband has left. Her daughter is dead and her son somewhere trying to forget. To it all—to this absence—she will have to go back.

From the safety of Jill's apartment, she organises for the glass to be replaced in the kitchen window at the house. And she speaks to Adam on the phone about bills. He is staying at his mother's. She is curt and tries to tie it up quickly but he sounds raw and despairing—not at all himself. He reminds her what a fiery temper she had when they first met. The time she stamped on his John Lennon sunglasses. She gives him a wry laugh. Neither suggests meeting up.

And when a new job comes in, her hand more or less healed, she packs her modest bag, buys a bottle of champagne and cooks a fish pie. They eat it from their laps, looking out over the silver water. She calls a cab at ten on a Tuesday night.

It feels better returning under cover of night. Is it the neighbours she wants to sneak past, or herself? Unlocking the heavy panelled front door she wishes she were dead—to have to come back here and live it all again. She thinks of Prometheus, but also Demeter, of course. How could she *not* come back to her haunted house?

With no one to please she throws her bag onto the floor and opens a bottle of wine. Puts a record on. She could stay up all night. Dance. Sing. Weep. No one and nothing to stop her.

She draws instead, spreading her materials—pencils, pastels, drawing pad, a saucer of water, an old cloth nappy, prints of Hutan—across the kitchen table.

She was going to be an artist, once; Adam a human rights lawyer. That they are only dull shades of these doesn't matter. This is not the thing she regrets. She still has the lines, the colour.

An hour passes. The new tiger's mouth yawns open. It isn't fierce—it is relaxed, sleepy even, bared teeth incidental. But in the bottom left corner something else is beginning to appear, prostrate on the ground. She pretends she doesn't know what it is, but she does.

She can't finish it quite yet. Finds her coat and keys and steps out around midnight; walks a few blocks to the 7-Eleven to buy cigarettes. They come in a plain black carton with a photo on the front of a foot in a mortuary, toe tagged. The government didn't factor in the nihilistic allure of such packaging. Back at the house she lights up in the kitchen. Starts trawling the web for tigers and comes—accidentally?—across a link to an article about a man savaged to death after launching himself into the tiger's enclosure at a Denmark zoo.

And what she thinks is: of course. Of course he did. It has been pushing at the edge of her consciousness, this very thing. To finally go to the heart of it—destroyed by the magnificence, the sheer ferocity, and the desperate, futile love.

The web trail leads to more suicide by tiger. She watches footage of a Singaporean cleaner throwing himself into the clutches of three cats while spectators with phone-cams gasp. In China—a depressed twenty-seven-year-old climbing a tree in order to leap in with the two white tigers. Apparently he wanted to feed them. Then: an attempted suicide at the Bronx Zoo. A young man casting himself off the tourist monorail and into the tiger's arms, surviving—miraculously—to explain that he wanted to be 'one with the tiger'.

To be one with the tiger. She draws some more and a figure appears in the bottom left corner of the paper. Limp, broken, but complete. It makes her weep.

She puts herself to bed on the couch that first night back, iPad and tea on the floor beside her; comforted by the hard lumpy cushions and the sense—however delusive—that she is just passing through.

One of the sisters goes down with the flu and Joe fills the extra shifts at the cafe, working the bar five nights out of seven. Not time enough for sleep but still the nurse drags him from bed to play until the midwinter sun rises. She likes best to leap, so they train at ground level using the architecturally considered volcanic rocks under the northern end of the bridge. The six-foot gap is a cinch for him to precision-jump, is something for the nurse to go at.

For his part, he is working to extend his cat leap, centimetre by hard-won centimetre, using the concrete platform. He is making eight feet. It is not enough.

'You're a good teacher,' she says, one of these pre-dawns. He is trying to help her with follow-through. Take-off is good—she has been working on strengthening the muscles in her feet—but she slows down in the air, like she doesn't really believe she can make it.

'Yeah? Well, you're top of the class. But you're still holding back. Once your feet leave the rock try to release into the jump. Use your mind to imagine yourself over. You're not going to hurt yourself.'

You're not going to hurt yourself. It echoes in his head. A train pummels over—early commuters with their deadlines and hot coffee breath—and under here, only them.

She nods slowly, big green eyes locked on to his, as if she finally gets it. 'I thought I was supposed to be in control . . . Don't hold back? I can do that. I'm not scared.'

On the next try, she almost makes it. Sails through the air, light as light, stumbles the landing, grazes her shins. And he thinks he could love her, and it is such a bad fucking idea.

Leaving so soon, she is barely even here, and she makes him remember—more than he wants.

How every couple of months they would split, after some perceived betrayal: his. It would happen when they were smashed. Jen would see him standing too close to another girl—laughing, or leaning in to catch something—and her thoughts would get fast and iron-hard (she would explain this later, his legs caught up in hers) until she could taste it in her mouth: rust; and hear it in her head: the roaring. And she would come for him, stealthily then full throttle, ready to tear out his heart.

The girl in question would melt away as Jen threw drinks, fists; friends trying and failing to talk her down. *I fucking hate you! How could you do this to me?* If he tried to hold her it was worse. He would shield his face; tell her she was a fucking lunatic. Walk away and she would follow. Hunt him down dark streets at two in the morning, wailing. A couple of times, cops were called. Once, his mother had to collect them from the lockup.

He never fought back but it made him weary, and pissed off. He didn't know what it was, this thing that happened. Jen would do anything for anyone but she had no faith.

They wouldn't speak for a week or two. *It's over,* they'd tell anyone who'd listen, and sometimes he would be glad. But he couldn't stay away from her, and she couldn't leave him be. Messages would be relayed, then he would go to her and they would make up, skin to skin. Swear there could be no one else.

Under the bridge he kisses the nurse. The willow where it all began weeps just out of sight. And he thinks she was right not to trust him: then or now.

10

Half-strength Dulux Paperbark: exceptional for its drabness. Just like his mother to try to camouflage the house. She could perch in a window looking out and no one would even know she was there.

After a fortnight of turning up every few days to sand and wash the surface of his childhood home, he has just cracked open the first fat tin, pouring a gutful of mauve-grey-beige into a black plastic pan. Slathers it on and hopes the rain will hold off—stupid time of year to be painting an exterior. His bad.

The paint goes on like a dubious dream and he gets caught up in the repetitive motion of the brushstrokes—the side-to-side sweep and the simple pleasure of covering something up. Two and a half hours glide by. Until his deltoids and brachioradialis ache and he is cross-eyed with looking at the slick surface.

His mother brings an unwanted mug of tea with a saucer of Assorted Creams and they sit together on the doorstep facing the quiet street.

He eats a few of the biscuits, fresh from the packet at least. And drinks the tea.

'I found your old hockey stick last week,' she says. 'Would you like it?'

'Not really.'

'And a box of your books from high school.'

'Give them to the op shop.'

'Are you sure? You might need them again.'

Tries to keep the exasperation out of his voice. 'What for?'

'The chemistry and physics books might still be useful . . . if you go to university, say.'

'Mum, they're high-school textbooks. I graduated from high school—yeah?' He stands up and stretches. Fuck. He could scale something bigger than a ladder right now. 'I'm going to get back to it. I have to get to work later.'

His mother goes back inside with the cup and plate and he remounts the ladder, thinking of the bridge, imagining the leap.

When he has finished one coat of the fascia—boards and shingles—he climbs down, leaves the brushes for his mother to clean. Catches a bus to Brunswick and runs the rest.

Showers out back and changes into his grim reaper, ready to put on music and light candles—get the stage set—but comes to a stop outside the kitchen. He can hear Lena on the other side of the door, singing—something in Ukrainian. He's heard her sing it before: a simple tune, sort of sad and wistful.

Stands still and listens. Mesmerised. Doesn't go in.

Later, when they are in motion, and he is moving fast and sure in and out of her kitchen, he compliments her new pixie haircut. It changes the lines of her face, makes it heart-shaped. She fries him a plate of sardines. He brings her a glass of red. She complains about Boss.

At the end of the night they clean up and go their separate ways.

The lean-to is dark.

Still hungry, he makes a peanut butter sandwich, eats, then turns out the light in his bedroom, awakens the screen and goes in. He knows it is becoming habitual again but he needs to see her—to know she was real. And with a few clicks, she is: estuarine eyes; the tiny gap between her front teeth. He remembers delicate hands in his; the tickle of her long black hair.

Tries to remember. The sense-memories are wearing thin.

He props the iPad up on the table beside the bed as he rolls a cigarette; wedging the window open with the shoebox; black-ice air. 'So what do you think of this house, anyway?' he asks her. 'You've never said. I would have thought you'd like the carpet, right?'

Inhales deeply and stares at her face until his vision distorts. She makes no comment. And his eye is drawn to the list of 'friends' online: Emily Dickinson is a green. On a whim he reaches into the void.

Hello.

After a couple of minutes she responds: *Joe.*

He butts out the cigarette.

Will you tell me who you are today?

This is easier don't you think?

Ha. Maybe for you—you know who I am.

Yes I'm sorry, you're right. Maybe it is easier for me.

Why?

It's complicated. I don't mean you any harm. Can I just be nobody for a little while?

I'll respect your anonymity for now.

How have you been?

And maybe it *is* easier for him too, because: *I'm scared I'm going to forget.*

Joe, you won't.

I am.

Well you're here, right, talking to me because you haven't forgotten.

Details are getting lost.

There is a pause.

We can't remember everything. That's just the work of time. She would understand.

No she wouldn't.

You're probably right.

So you're a fan of Dickinson too.

Jen and I used to memorise poems together.

Aha, so you were in English Lit with her. Don't worry I don't have a class list.

We would throw lines at each other and try to work out what stuff meant, you know, the transience of life and the immortality of art etc.

Sounds like you really nailed it.

She was better at it than me.

She was good at a lot of things.

Yeah she was. But she wasn't perfect. Let's not make her into a saint—she would hate that.

Heaven forbid.

She could be moody as hell.

Stubborn.

Do you remember what she did to that poor girl with the pet rat?

Ha. She felt bad about that.

There is a long pause and he thinks she has gone. Then: *It's late and I have to work tomorrow but it was good to talk. Those details you said get lost—this brings them back.*

Night, Emily.

Night, Joe.

He closes the message window and looks back to Jen. 'So what do you make of that then? Who's your friend?'

And it's a fancy but he could swear she is more animated, looking at him properly now. Enigmatic, sure, but they are smiling right at one another.

To have spoken to someone else who loved her.

Logs out and shuts down; stretches out in the dark; hoping and hoping-not that the nurse will come.

She appears when the hours are timeless and he is half in dream. In her navy scrubs, name badge on her chest, stethoscope swinging. Still wearing her tool belt with shiny scissors, forceps, tweezers, fob watch, pocket calculator, pencil, eraser, cheap ballpoint pen.

He takes it all off; she reaches for him. Noiselessly.

Under the covers she whispers of her day—her night. Road trauma du jour—more lines going in than a fibre-optic network; decent chance of recovery. But, too: the pointless hourly obs on the girl with no brain function. She fought with her boyfriend, apparently, but it is rare to find a girl hanging. They usually take a softer way out. Pills; a fall; car running but going nowhere.

'There's nothing there, but we can't turn her off because she's breathing unaided.'

'So what happens?'

'We wait. Talk to the family. Etcetera, etcetera.'

'But she isn't in pain?'

'She isn't anything. She is nowhere.' The nurse curls up, facing away from him.

'Is it so bad to be nowhere?' He strokes her arm. 'You're cold. Come here.'

But she pulls away. 'Yes it's bad. Limbo sucks.' Minutes pass, or hours. She rolls back to him. 'Let's go out. I want to practise.'

'You're beautiful,' he whispers. 'But I need to sleep.'

Painting the house, working the bar; he has to open up the cafe in the morning for the sisters. They occupy such contrary worlds; sometimes it feels as if there is a bodily cost to each stolen hour.

'Sleep is boring.' She yawns. 'Take it from me. I've spent the night surrounded by the living dead.'

He tries to hold her but she goes.

———

First Thursday back: locking up her bike in a cold spit of rain; flashing her membership card at the girl pink-cheeked in the ticket box exuding common sense. Detour to Meerkat Manor, where orange plastic tables have married the bird-of-paradise surrounds, to have her keep-cup filled with coffee. She celebrates her return with two of the lightweight coconut cookies, though they wouldn't satisfy an ant.

Bearing morning tea along the main path that divides the twin plane trees, to the chime of the bellbirds; past Lemur Island and onto the Elephant Trail. The lush otherworldliness of it: stepping over fat puddles, embraced by the animated, glistening-green foliage. Brief pause at the otters, really just to draw it all out: the wet weasels are in hiding. And then over Tiger Bridge, pausing to glance down at the fetid green water, and the Indonesian sign to *beware!*

Oh, how she has missed this.

How she has missed the cats.

She can hear the beating of her own heart as she approaches the first viewing window. It is like manna—to arrive again knowing they will be here, still alive and indomitable, more or less. And today it is—yes!—Indrah, stretched out on a bed of fresh hay beneath the low wooden shelter, out of the rain. The tiger looks up, fixes Elise briefly through the glass, before returning to the sprucing of her spectacular pelt.

Released, mirroring the cat, Elise drops to a languid squat in front of the glass. Sips her coffee and devours the cookies.

She can feel the joy and relief of being back in the looseness of her folded limbs. She used to squat like this when the children were small and running back and forth from the safety of her arms. She recalls how her body felt infinitely strong and her heart infinitely soft, as if she were built, blood, bone and sinew, to love and protect. As gratifying a feeling as she has ever known, that surety in her bent haunches as the children came and went. Fleeting moments where all the colours in the world shimmied into perfect alignment—unbounded blues and grass-greens; the lurid dyes of their cheap little outfits; the barley-cream of their sandwich bread. Here, with Indrah, it all comes flooding back.

Until a member of staff strides by, mouth to walkie-talkie, deep in logistics; something about a lemur running amok. And Elise, in coming to, wonders briefly how she might appear to one in passing. Would the young man in khaki see at a glance that all this means too much? Her eyes a little too bright, too focused? Might he not mutter into his walkie-talkie: *Think we've got a live one here. Send in the team.*

She grins gamely at Indrah who is not cursed with this apish self-awareness, though a body like hers would go for half a million—more—on the Chinese black market. Eyeballs to cure epilepsy; whiskers for sore tooth. Tiger wine to get things sexy. A paw hung over the entrance to chase away ghosts. And most prized: the heart, the eating of which is said to bestow courage. Who wouldn't want to be more tigerish?

The rain has not eased but the cat eventually bores with the beauty treatment. After all, there are no battle wounds to disinfect. She sets out to patrol her diminutive territory, stopping to sniff and then claw at the solid trunk of the plane tree, padding down to the water's edge to scan the short horizon before heading to the fence between the enclosure and sleeping quarters. She sets to pacing the boundary line, carving out a figure eight in the mud, emitting the odd guttural call to her brothers.

Elise moves around to the bench seat and huddles deeper into her coat. She wonders if the tiger will ever be given the opportunity to mate. Where once there was courtship and displays of strength before a private meeting, now there is a human whose job it is to keep the tiger book. Flitting from zoo to zoo across the globe conducting spot checks, making matches between captive cats. But there are not cages enough to permit all tigers these rights. And cats born in captivity cannot be released into the wild. Will the matchless Indrah get lucky?

Tiger mother: teeth that crush femurs like breadsticks carry mewling cubs without breaking skin; mace-like paws employed in gentle cavorting. That excoriating tongue applied lightly to baby fur. Perfect strength meets perfect love. But even a tiger mother is only able to protect her young up to a point. There will be moments when her back is turned.

At midday Elise bids Indrah farewell and winds her way back out into the world. Unlocks her bike and pushes off, riding fast into the centre of the deepest puddles. Mud up her old blue jeans. She has work to do—and another job lined up after that—but first she will treat herself to a swim and maybe she'll buy fish for dinner, an *Art Almanac* to find out what's showing, her very own bottle of gin.

⎯

They get to AAMI stadium ten minutes before kick-off; buy hotdogs and find seats. Wrapped in coats in the glacial night air, tens of thousands of excited humans face the floodlit field as if a UFO were about to alight. In this setting Joe gets the draw of anonymity. It's nice to blend into the masses and disappear, personal history erased. He tries to translate this to Deck.

'Yeah.' Deck smirks. 'We're all just your average Joe.'

'Ha. Funny. So what happened? Your mum said you weren't supposed to come because you were suspended. It's lucky I'm so charming.'

'Deadbeat mongrel Mr Tyers, he has mashed-potato ears.'

Players start running out onto the field. Applause is strident and overegged: the New Zealand contingent far outnumbered by Hearts fans. Someone lets off a flare in the membership section and the red smoke brings security men running.

'What did you do to Mr Tyers?' The hotdogs warm their hands and guts.

'Nothing.'

''Course you didn't.'

'You must have been suspended, back in the day, right?' Deck says eventually.

'What makes you say that?'

'Duh. It's only obvious.'

'What is?'

'You know. That you used to be a badass.'

Joe looks straight ahead and smiles. All the effort he goes to and now this. The whistle goes.

'Well? It's true isn't it?'

Joe shrugs.

'What's the big deal?'

'Watch the game.'

'What'd you do? Set fire to your school or something?'

When Joe only laughs Deck frowns and slowly shakes his head, in perfect mimicry of every one of the despairing adults in his world.

'Okay. I was suspended once or twice. Truancy, petty theft, stuff like that.'

'Sheeeesh. That's it?'

Phoenix has taken possession. The ball zigzags downfield, player to player in a neat set piece, evading interference, until their key striker scores a perfect header goal. A great 'boo' rumbles through the stadium.

'I had a small argument,' Deck says.

'With your teacher?'

'*No*. Guy in my class.'

'Over what?'

Deck shrugs.

'The girl?'

'Maybe.'

'Who won the small argument?'

'Who do you think?'

It is like looking in the mirror and Joe smiles despite himself. 'How badly did you hurt him?'

'Broken nose.'

He should say something about using peaceful means to resolve conflict, blah blah, maybe a quote from Gandhi. 'You dickhead.'

'He's the dickhead.'

'What happened with the girl?'

'We broke up.'

'Shit. Sorry to hear that.'

'Wevs.'

At halftime Phoenix are leading one–nil. They queue for ice-creams and eat them wandering around the curved interior corridors of the stadium. Everywhere they look there are fathers with sons. Joe wonders if Deck notices.

Maybe he does: 'My dad rang. He said I could go up when the weather is better.'

'Cool.'

'I thought maybe you could come, seeing as you haven't got any friends. Or only weird ones. He wants to take me fishing.'

'You need a driver, huh?'

'Yeah, that's it.'

'Sure, I'll come.'

'She's not going out with the other guy either.'

'No?'

'She's psycho.'

Hearts come back in the second half and take the next two goals to win. At the final whistle, tens of thousands of fans jump up and down on their seats, wielding their red and white scarves and flags, claiming the victory for their very own. Deck and Joe holler with the rest of them.

11

After a double shift at the cafe he pulls up outside the laun-dromat late afternoon midweek; slides the key out from between the two bricks. Some idiot forgot to empty their pockets of coins so one of the driers next door clinks on every clank.

'Joey!' Sanjay's Lucille Ball. 'Up here, Joey!'

Goes inside and drags off his boots; pulls on a beanie; passes the lean-to and out the back door; cluck-cluck-cluck go the chickens; climbs the ladder in his socks.

Jack and Sanjay are sprawled either side of a bottle of cheap Prosecco. All semester break they have lolled around the house like baby walruses. 'You called me up here for this?'

'He got into the law,' Sanjay explains earnestly.

Jack looks up to gauge Joe's reaction. Joe grins. 'Congratulations. I knew you'd get in. You deserve it.'

'Classes start next week. I've got like a fucking shitload of reading. This is my last night of being bad.'

Joe has a screenshot of all that is passing him by; it is technicoloured. But what's so bad about black and white? At least he is alive.

The sun is slowly falling and he is alive. He reaches for the Prosecco.

'Bro?' Sanjay holds the bottle out of reach. 'You don't drink, bro.'

'That's very sweet but he's an adult and this is a celebration. Give it to him,' Jack says.

Sanjay stows the bottle behind him. 'I'm going to make you a ginger refresher, my man.'

Jack guffaws.

'Shut up, dickwad,' Sanjay snaps.

Joe reaches around Sanjay and grabs the bottle, takes a pull straight from the neck. It's all sugar and fizz. 'I'm going to go buy something better,' he says, standing, stretching up onto his toes. 'You only transfer into Law once, right?'

'YOTILO,' Jack drawls.

Joe backs down the ladder. Sanjay is still frowning.

'Promise I won't mess up your shoes when I start hurling.'
He smiles.

'Nothing wrong with taking pride in your footwear,' Sanjay
mutters.

Joe comes back ten minutes later with two bottles of Chilean
cab sav, another glass and Jack's guitar. Hands Jack the guitar
and pours.

'Yeah, no, *this* is good,' says Jack, swishing the wine around
his mouth.

Sanjay gives him a death stare. 'You are a tosser.'

Jack plays blues chords and Joe closes his eyes, the alcohol
warming him. Maybe he just needs to stop thinking. His
mother's eyes. Todd's hands. The nurse. The jump. And Jen.
Always Jen.

'*Sitting on the roof, my best mates and me,*' Jack sings.
'*There is no other place I'd rather be. Going to make me a law
degree-eee-eee, going to make me a lawyer, old man, you'll see.*'

A couple of girls look up from the pavement outside the
laundromat and laugh. 'Too young,' says Jack dismissively.

Sanjay disappears down the ladder in disgust. Soon after,
the Bollywood starts up beneath them. Joe groans.

'Let's go out,' Jack says. 'Find some action.'

The last centimetre of sun is peeking over the rooftops.

'Sure.' Joe is out of practice; he is half-cut already. The night feels coldly alive.

When it's fully dark they climb down, piss onto the lemon tree, find phones, money, travel cards. Sanjay brushes his beautiful white teeth, ready to forgive and forget.

They jump on a tram, loud, laughing, and then walk up to Brunswick Street.

There is an old-timey band playing at Bar Open. They buy beer; malty and dark it goes down like wet treacle. Stand in the corner talking shit. Casting around. Jack throws his arms around his two friends. 'I'll do all your jobs pro bono.'

'Bullshit,' Sanjay says. 'You'd charge your grandmother.'

'I'd charge *your* grandmother,' Jack says. Pointlessly.

They all laugh.

One of the girls behind the bar is pretty. Blonde hair upswept, a bit like Lena's before she cut it. She makes eyes at Joe throughout the night and at closing asks if they want to stay on. A lock-in. He hasn't done this in years.

'Why did I stop drinking?' he asks.

'Bro, you were a little bit fucked up,' Sanjay says.

'But you're all right now, yeah?' Jack adds. 'And we're watching over you.'

Someone puts on a playlist and the beer keeps pouring. Joe talks to the bar girl. It is not that hard. They have a lot in common: working in a bar. Sanjay is talking to the ginger-haired sylph from the band; she is putty in his hands. Jack has met some guy from uni and they are gesticulating furiously. Probably opining about the state of the criminal courts. Now that he is a law man.

Then she is on his lap. How did that happen? He thinks fleetingly of the nurse but haven't they kept it quiet for a reason? What is it they have, anyway? This strange formless thing that thrives on half-light; the way she comes and goes without warning or explanation.

Slides a hand up the girl's leg. 'You're cute,' he says in her ear.

'So are you.'

Kissing a little. Talking. Laughing. Touching. Too much for in here. He has a hard-on.

'Want to go to your place?' she says.

'What about yours?'

'I live at home.'

There is something wrong with this plan but he is too fucked to remember what.

Taxi: groping. Stumbling past the laundromat all lit up, through the front door and into his room. She pushes him down onto the bed. He pulls off her dress. Reaching up through the haze to grip her warm flesh. He can hardly feel it, but somehow they manage to have sex.

Restless hours pass before the door swings slowly open. He looks up.

The nurse: from the girl to him and back, eyes like green coppers. Backing out without a sound.

He doesn't move, or say a thing. The bar girl sighs and rolls over.

Climbs out of bed. Queasy, and his brain hurts. Pulls on tracksuit pants and a long-sleeved t-shirt. Laces on his Feiyue. He will warm up fast out there.

He should wake the girl lying in his bed, say something. What kind of an arsehole. Writes a note instead.

In the corridor he can hear Jack snoring. Looks down towards the lean-to, hesitates, moving his weight from one foot to the other, then steps out through the front door, deposits the key.

Drops. Breathes: One. Two. Three. Four. Five. Leaps.

Goes hard to the corner. In the playground, a running jump up the slide then turning midway, hands-free, holding the centre of gravity at his core, and pushing off with his feet to jump back down into a precision landing. *Lache* on the monkey bars. Exiting the park with an underbar and a series of five forward rolls over unforgiving cement.

In the laneway, along the rooftops, it's like he's running towards the rising sun.

Back then—before: sex was a miracle. They were immortal and every day was infinity.

Waking to the warm, whispering fact of her in his single bed in his boyhood room. The strip of black-and-white headshots from the train station photo booth pinned below the flying Maradona: 1. Winking. 2. Swooning. 3. Her laughing profile, looking out. 4. She is pulling him in, behind the black curtain, for a long wet kiss.

He'd only been shaving about a year. Todd had turned up one night with a razor and brush; stood side by side with him at the bathroom mirror. Showed him how to follow the lines of his jaw, firm and steady, scraping upwards under the chin. Later, Jen wanted a go too, part of playing Mums and Dads. She put him on a chair in the kitchen at her house when no one else was home and draped a towel around his neck. Lathered him up. Gave him the full service.

Why is it that he thinks so much about the sex? As if in those moments they were fucking, death was already there, and they were holding it off with their bare hands.

She used to pick him up from soccer training sometimes. He'd started playing again after they got together. She'd get there early and stand at the edge to watch. *Why is it always so windy in this park? The rest of the city might be Buenos Aires but this little park is blowing a gale.* He'd wrap his slicker around her and they'd walk back to his place. Thirteen blocks. Make hot chocolate. Watch TV. She would chat with his mum, all grown up, about music and books and politics.

He'd look for her at the edge of the oval even when she wasn't there.

She got it into her head once that she had to meet his dad. Was she going to charm him better? He brushed it off until one morning at the lockers she showed him the ad on her phone for cut-price flights to Brisbane. She was flushed. *I'm going to buy us tickets! I've got enough in the bank. We could go at Easter!* He had to explain that he wasn't going without an invitation and even then. She couldn't get it. She wouldn't. *Come on, Joe! He's your dad.*

After school that day they had a fight at his house; he told her to fuck off back to her perfect life and she did, slamming the front door behind her. Ten minutes later she returned. It was one of only two times he cried in front of her. They went to Queenscliff for Easter with his mum and stayed at the youth hostel.

Trying to shape him into something that fit: nagging him to do homework. She was all *A+* and *Excellent work, Jennifer!*

while he did well enough. He didn't want to be a hotshot lawyer like her dad—was that it? Was it her dad she had to please? She taped the periodic table to his bedroom wall. He took it down.

But she also liked to get bent. It was like when they went to the pool to play strangers—she wanted to try stuff to see what would emerge. Coke was fun when they could get it, sometimes an E. She didn't like the chanciness of acid. Drink was dicey right from the start. Even without the jealousy she couldn't hold it.

Once, after she'd made herself sick on tequila: *I am never never doing that again, you hear me?*

Yeah right. He got her lemon cordial and let her rest her head on his chest. Dragged his fingers through the knots in her long black hair.

It's your fault, she said. *You always make it better. So I forget.*

12

Elise shoots off the latest job with an invoice and drafts an email to line up the next; won't send until she's checked costings with the printer. There is another small job—a logo—she could knock off tomorrow. But for now: puts on a Nina Simone record and turns it up loud. Wheels the vacuum cleaner out of the laundry and unwinds the cord; plugs it into the wall and switches it on—vroom! And then freezes in the middle of the living room with the sucker vibrating in her hand. She is filling this big empty house with flurry and for what?

To hell with the completion clean. The fine coat of dust on the surfaces and floors, the fried-egg grease around the stove, the smears of soap in the bathroom basin—there is no one here who gives a shit. No one is going to come home tonight and say, *Oh, now* this *is nice—would you take a look at this place?* Had anyone *ever* said anything like that?

A still life—that's what's on offer here. She might as well take it.

Wheels the vacuum cleaner back into the laundry and shuts the door; turns the music down a little—Nina subdues. The rest of the day is hers.

She retrieves the roll of cotton canvas from the linen closet, where she stuffed it last week after a rash visit to the art supply shop, then sets about clearing the table, moving her laptop and iPad, colour palettes, paperwork, empty bowl and cup to the kitchen counter. Wipes the tabletop down with a damp cloth and gives it a minute to dry while she goes upstairs for the tools stored in a dusty box under her bed.

Downstairs, she slides the plastic covering off the canvas and pauses to savour the coarse material beneath her fingers. It has been a long time. About fifteen years.

From the toolbox she takes shears that once belonged to her grandmother, who made all her own clothes. She uses these to cut off a length of canvas, measuring by sight. She has bought a bunch of stretchers, too; maybe one day she'll start making her own again.

Starting in the middle of one side, she turns the raw edge of the canvas over to create a small hem then nails it to the stretcher, hammering the first tack dead centre. Shuns the staple gun Adam gave her one Christmas. She always did prefer carpet tacks, a fresh packet emptied into the rusty old tobacco tin.

She holds a bunch of the tacks in her mouth. And it's like it was yesterday—the taste of the metal and the promise it holds. Moves to the opposite side of the stretcher and, using canvas pliers for leverage, pulls the material taut to tack down the centre. Repeats with the remaining two sides.

Pauses to make coffee, setting the small espresso maker on a low flame. Flips the record.

Returning to the original side of the stretcher she hammers in a tack at a time, moving outward and left from the middle. Has always done it the same way, since uni. Turns the stretcher to the diagonally opposite side and uses the pliers to pull the canvas tight, tacking to the left. Speeding up now—you never forget, it's like lacing a shoe. Continues until all the edges are in place, moving from one opposing section to the next to ensure the tension is even. At the corners she folds the excess material and fastens it neatly, three tacks per corner.

Pours the coffee.

And out of long-ago habit—ritual—taps the centre of the stretched canvas with her fingertips. It sounds as it should: like a drum. No ripples. Just right.

The process reminds her of making bread, something she has not done since Adam left. Or, more abstractly, the long haul of raising a child: the hope that if you take enough care with the preparation, and don't rush any steps, you'll turn out something fine. And she did. She surely did.

She spreads a layer of newspaper down on the table and uses a coin to lever the lid off the shiny tin of oil primer. Recalls the hot reek of cheap rabbit-skin glue in her first studio. It only needs one coat of this new stuff. She takes a thick brush and paints it on. In a couple of days the canvas will be ready to go.

Yesterday she found the easel, tucked deep under the house. Wriggled in on her belly, shivering with cold, and dragged it out; brushed off the cobwebs. The old stains and smears of paint are as familiar as a map of one's hometown. She left it resting against the side of the house to be washed by the rain.

And now, leaving the canvas to dry at one end of the table, she takes the cover off the plastic tub full of grubby chewed-up little tubes. Her oils—beloved colours she had almost forgotten. Viridian green, raw umber, rose madder. Hard little nipples of colours once mixed on the back of a faded plastic ice-cream lid. She picks them up and puts them down, the colours—remembering—but she's going to need a whole new set. And tucked in among the paints are familiar old rags, just waiting here, mutely wadded, made from her dead mother's sheets.

Dead mother, dead daughter, she is starting to get what this means: that she is bereft, yes, but also . . . accountable to no one. Perhaps after all there is something to be made from this.

Leaving everything just as it is, she turns off the stereo, locks up and heads out. She is going to see Carl. He was unfazed, Adam said, about the separation. In the grand scheme of things, as her daughter would have said, whatever. She can't wait to rest her eyes on his handsome face.

And tomorrow is Thursday again.

―

For a week the nurse does not come; he hears her padding down the hallway like a cat. He works, paints his mother's house, plays soccer in the mud with Deck, and avoids the lean-to. Wants to give her space; and has to work out what he means to say.

He has been going to the bridge in the early evenings before work, after the schoolkids have gone home to hot dinners. The bridge can be relied upon: its scale and solidity extend a permanent invitation. Climbing up onto the orange steel girder and sidling along the ledge, disturbing pigeons and mynahs as they nestle down to their long winter nights. Sometimes a pair of welcome swallows.

He has grown comfortable with standing in position, halfway across the underside, toes hanging over the edge. Likes to look downstream through the cheese-hole and see and not-see the grey footbridge, keeping something just out of reach. Is no longer rattled by trains when they roll overhead. Some days he thinks he could make it across to the pillar; others, it looks like a death wish.

Requiring every major muscle group, the cat leap works when the gap is too great for a simple jump. The principles are straightforward but the practice is a work of art.

Take-off will have to be calm and measured but also explosive, or he will not make it. Leading with the upper body there will be time in the air to correct posture, bringing knees forward to land feet first on the vertical side of the pillar followed instantaneously by upper body, hands gripping the top lip, using the momentum of the jump to pull up into the mount.

Landing should be easier to control from a standing jump— if he can make the distance. Arms and legs need to be pliable as he hits the pillar: if the impact is too great he'll bounce off;

too little and he won't have the impetus to make the mount. If his feet land too low he won't get a good grip. If they land too high he will fall backwards.

Every part of the move has to be practised until it is solid and then sewn together into one fluid sequence. Practised and practised until it is seamless, until nothing can go wrong, and even then. He has to be ready.

He is getting closer to making the distance on the concrete platform under the northern end of the bridge but follow-through is shambolic. Has to be patient: this cannot be rushed. But the jump is pressing up in him. He is dreaming about it at night, running it through. Already doing it in his mind, he has to wait for his body to catch up.

After work on Friday night he catches the nurse on the darkened pavement at the back of the laundromat. Doesn't see her, and then she is right there.

'Joe.' Evenly.

His heart trips. In jeans and boots, her pale skin, black hair all scruffy and soft, she glows.

'The other morning,' he says quickly. 'The girl. I want to explain. Could we talk?'

'Can't. Gotta go.'

'You're not going to work?'

'Is it any of your business?'

'No, I guess not.'

'I'm not going to do the whole jealous thing,' she goes on. 'I'm too old for that.'

'Yes, you're being very mature.'

'But you can still fuck off.'

She walks east up the side street, disappearing into the night. He pulls the front door closed behind him.

Sanjay is in his room, laughing, and there is a girl's voice— maybe the fiddle player from the band? Sanjay seemed almost serious about that. No sign of Jack—probably at the library or at his mum's getting fed.

He makes coffee and goes to his room. Lies on the bed with the iPad to watch clips of cat leaps, studying the push-off, sifting through endless examples and tutorials to find something he might tweak.

And without much thought he opens Facebook, in the background.

Within minutes, a message in the bottom right corner.

Are you there?

Yeah.

Are you always there?

Are you?

Times we live in I guess . . .

Well yeah.

Where do you live these days—still in Melbourne?

Why would I tell you that?

Sorry, it just struck me you could be anywhere, you know—maybe you got a scholarship to play soccer in Brazil or something . . . you were good.

Ha. No. What about you? Are you holed up in some garret in Castlemaine with your quill?

I'm still in the city. Haven't been anywhere exciting.

Last night I dreamt about her. She was running up the road in bare feet and she looked happy, she was laughing, but I was worried about her feet.

I'm sorry. Shit. That's beautiful and sad.

I was worried she was going to get glass in her feet. And there was a taxi on its way, that's why she was excited. I think she was going off on some big adventure.

Her feet are okay, Joe. She's not in any pain.

Her feet aren't okay, Emily Dickinson. She doesn't have any feet.

Nothing.

Nothing.

Fuck you and your platitudes anyway, he thinks. Whoever you fucking are.

He navigates to Jen's page. Come down, see the incredible pixelated girl! Her status still: In a relationship. And for the first time this bothers him. Will he never be free?

He rolls a cigarette and burns his finger on the match. 'Is this better?' he mutters to her smiling face. 'Now I've fucked it up with the sexy nurse?'

But she can't fight back, can't defend her territory. All that shit he hated, all the drama, he aches for it. Lifts his left hand and hits the wall above his head as hard as he can. Pain vibrates down his arm like blue notes on a guitar.

He wants to be rid of her. He wants to never let her go.

'I'm sorry,' he whispers. How many times does he have to say it? 'I'm sorry you are not here.'

Three years and he still cannot fathom that nothing he does or doesn't do will make any difference at all.

Ten minutes later: *You're right not to mince words, Joe, there is too much of that, and now you've got me thinking how much she loved being barefoot.*

This time he shuts it down.

He could walk up the road and buy a bottle of whisky, but the desire is not really there.

So he lies in the dark and watches the YouTube clip of the Tokyo guy; watches it over and over till he can close his eyes and he is there jumping alongside, tower to office tower.

The seven-legged huntsman is in the far corner of the ceiling, bedding down too. Each to his own wild dreams.

In the days and weeks after, they mourned her by getting smashed. Fitting, really. Her death was an accelerant. Teetering on the precipices of new adult lives, headed in all different directions, the group held beyond its use-by date that they might rage and grieve together.

It was as close to comfort as he could get. Everyone there except her. They rose like a pack to his nihilistic howl, and he lost himself in their embrace, where she was known and would be remembered.

About a month after, they caught a bus to someone's aunt's beach house on the Great Ocean Road. Pink stucco: four bedrooms. Carport with a pool table. Boxes of pasta and bottled sauce, cereal, beer. So grown up.

On the first night they went down to the beach. A few of them set to building a raft out of driftwood, fastened with string. One of the girls had brought a photo of Jen and they lay this on the raft with a straggle of wildflowers and a skirt the girl had borrowed and never given back—something semi-formal, might have been Jen's mother's. They doused the lot in kerosene and then, as the sun fell behind the ocean, they set the raft alight and pushed it out to sea.

Joe refused to participate. Sat further back on the beach, mute and scowling—hating it, this send-off. Why did they want to send her away? Only rejoined them later to raid the aunt's liquor cabinet and snort lines of someone's cocaine.

During that long wiped-out weekend, one of Jen's friends came to his bed when everyone else was sleeping. She took off all her clothes and slid in. It made him cry again. They had fast bad sex.

It had to end—the memorialising and group hugs. Because while their friends were devastated they were also glad it had not been them. In part, in those early days, they were rejoicing. They were only human. Jen's absence called attention to the miracle of their own mortal breath misting the mirror.

As they dispersed into new jobs, university, relationships, travel, he deferred his course and lived off his mother, not showing for the interviews lined up by Centrelink. Made a couple of older friends with a taste for tragedy and money to spend. But every girl he fucked, every hangover. Every car he bounced up and down on like a tin trampoline. Every bottle he shattered and held to his own throat. Only moved her further away.

The thing was he wished it *had* been him. And because the breath came in and out of his mouth he avoided the mirror.

Then one sunny afternoon Todd banged on his door while he was sleeping. He was already living behind the laundromat. Working at the cafe to pay the rent, getting fucked up every night, he had been ignoring his mother's calls. She was ready to call the police.

Okay, son, that's enough, Todd said, burning toast and coffee. *What you are doing is an insult to Jen's memory.*

Was it that Todd called him son, or was it the idea of Jen seeing him like this? He got out of bed that afternoon and followed Todd to the nursery, where he was put to work sorting through boxes of seed packets, discarding those past their best.

Got the second job. Stopped drinking. Hooked up with Deck. Gave up Facebook. Learnt to run, climb and jump.

He would keep it simple. Honour her memory.

But if he could just be with her one last time. Feel the contours of her body with the tips of his fingers; smell the back of her neck where it was warm and private; taste her; look into her clever eyes and explain to her how desperately sorry he was. He is.

That he accused her of sabotage and told her he'd had enough. That he didn't just hang in there like she needed him to. That night. Sorry beyond belief he didn't tell her one last time that he loved her.

That he pushed open that heavy door into the building stairwell with the flickering light, to take the safe way down. Leaving her to that strange chilled apartment on the fifth floor, with people who didn't care about her—most of whom she'd never met—and the shit electronic music turned up too loud.

Sorry he boarded a tram and went home to his single bed in his boyhood room where he slept soundly—relieved, even—as she lay dying.

13

She invites Jill and another old uni friend, Tom, for Sunday dinner. Cleans up a bit and makes chicken soup and plum cake, lights a fire in the living room. There is a layer of thick black sludge on top of the sourdough starter at the back of the fridge—it looks more dead than alive—but the house itself is warm and close to welcoming.

Before they arrive she drags the easel, paints and paraphernalia into the laundry, out of sight. She is working on a new tiger. With the switch to oils the cat seems to have woken up a bit; in big messy strokes it has become more menacing and unpredictable. The prostrate figure is in the background now, like something discarded. It remains grey and inanimate.

There is a clang of the old brass knocker, and Tom, with a bunch of sea holly. He kisses her cheek and she flusters. She has been noticing these moments of intense longing; she just doesn't know who it is she is longing for. Stuffs the flowers in a vase that's too small, opens the wine and asks Tom to choose music. Soon after, Jill turns up.

Her friends sit at the kitchen counter, where Adam would perch after work, while she slices bought bread and chops parsley. They carry the soup to the living room to sit by the fire, balancing bowls on their laps.

They traverse the usual terrain. Discussing the flaccid state of politics and getting nostalgic about their own switched-on youth, laughing at themselves as they do it. Tom has new stories from the think tank. Jill workshops her long service. There is more wine and with the world shut out, they regress to earlier selves: the gift of old friends. They eat cake with their fingers and Jill shares high-school gossip, abuses of power, the usual.

The tone changes when Tom talks about his marriage break-up five years ago. He is offering Elise an opportunity she declines. Is it because she remembers having a crush on Tom once? She wonders now if she is imagining the slight tautness between them. Probably just social awkwardness—they only catch up every year or two.

After he has left, Jill pours another glass. 'I'm sleeping over,' she announces. 'Curriculum day tomorrow.'

'Yeah!'

'We can stay up all night watching movies.'

'Perfect.' Elise chucks her the guide. 'I've been smoking.'

'I know. I could smell it when I came in. Go for your life. I will enjoy it passively.'

'On top of everything else, it looks like a midlife crisis.'

'You might as well. Get it out of the way. Two-for deal.'

'Tom's still cute, isn't he?'

Jill makes a face. 'Too thin. He was never my type. But I think he's still got the hots for you.' Jill pokes the fire. 'What's happening with Adam?'

At the mention of Adam, Elise's second adolescence dissolves. Still, she lights a cigarette from the open flames. 'We're not really speaking.'

'It's been, what, six weeks?'

'Seven, almost eight.'

'Surely you're going to have to talk at some point?'

'I suppose so. He actually said he was looking for someone we could go and see together. If I was willing. Can you believe it?'

'Of course I can. I'm sure he's lost without you. How is he enduring being at his mother's?'

'She cooks his favourite dinners and otherwise leaves him alone. She's his perfect wife.'

'Has he mentioned the other woman?'

'No. And I haven't asked. I have my dignity.'

'Don't be too hasty in writing him off, that's all I'm saying.' Jill stretches out on the floor, puts a cushion under her head. Sighs. 'You know, I don't think I've ever really been in love. Like, really, deeply, walk-over-hot-coals love.'

'Vince?'

'Ha! Seriously now. I remember watching my goddaughter and thinking, wow, she's got something at seventeen I've never had. That was a bit confronting sometimes.'

Elise nods. Tears happen out of her, sort of effortlessly. 'Thank you for being so special to her.'

'I loved *her*. Love her.'

'I know.'

Jill asks, careful now, 'Have you spoken to the boy?'

'I haven't seen him since the first anniversary when he was drunk and insufferable. What would I say?' She flicks the cigarette butt into the fire. 'Let's talk about something else.'

'Hey, I just had another thought about long service—what about India? Properly—the whole *Darjeeling Express*. The Ganges and the Taj Mahal. *And*, I was thinking, you should come. Even if it's just for a couple of weeks.'

'Ohhh! I don't think I can afford it, with the separation, and the fucking mortgage . . . Great idea, though.'

'You could start putting money in a jar. And we could stay at hostels. Think of all those spangled gods, the music. Just what a weary soul needs.'

'Next year?'

'Yeah, and, *oh*, aren't there lots of tigers there?'

———

'Bro, the smoke, bro! You know house rules.'

They are in the kitchen washing up two weeks' worth of dishes that have begun to putrefy.

'Yeah, no, thought it was going straight out the window.' Joe smiles.

'Nothing gets by this.' Sanjay taps his regal nose. 'And you know my father . . . He's coming next week to clean the gutters. My mother will cook for us.'

Joe scrapes at the crust of week-old batter in their single mixing bowl; it is blackening around the edges. Sanjay's new girlfriend made pancakes. 'I can't believe your sensitive nose doesn't object to the rot. Look at this. It's unsavoury. Next time just rinse the bowl. It'd take about five seconds.'

'Ah, we are young men with many large responsibilities.'

'Huh. Like getting stoned and having sex with your girlfriend.'

Sanjay splays his hands. 'A man has to do.'

'A man has to. I understand.' That Sanjay and Jack always had mothers at the ready, and that he is the sucker keeping the house from ruin. 'So how's it going, anyway?'

'Joey, it is so *fine*. Have you seen her? She is like Cleopatra.'

'Sanjay, she's not. I like her, though. She's funny.'

Seeing the fiddler formally now, Sanjay moves back and forth between their houses—because women can get psyched out by too much majestic male energy. On the weekends the two of them have been ploughing a new bed in the backyard, sewing seed for spring, bringing in bouquets of silverbeet and pockets full of eggs to turn into frittata. She plays music while he cooks. It is dizzying, almost painful, to watch. Makes the thing with the nurse look like gossamer. And she is, anyway, avoiding him.

Jack has fallen out of circulation too, now he has started with *the law*. Up late with the optional as well as required reading, he has taken to wearing wire-rimmed spectacles. Sanjay claims they are plain glass. He hogs the round table in the living room, drinks their milk, shares less. He is on a mission and they all know the stakes are high.

And Joe? Yesterday, he finished the first coat of his mother's house. He will do one more. She embraced him with bony wings and tried to give him some money, which he refused.

'You will learn to love Emma,' Sanjay declares. 'Because you are my best friend. Ah, but not too much love! Just the right amount, yeah?'

Joe doesn't answer.

So Sanjay loops the damp tea towel around Joe's neck like he is a prizefighter. 'You okay, Joey? Something on your mind, brother?'

Joe shrugs off the wet towel—remembering the towel around his neck in Jen's kitchen, her wielding the razor—and nods towards the window. 'It's cold. It's dark.' It's kind of fucking lonely.

'Here, let me.' Sanjay takes the scourer from him in an act of great courage and sacrifice. 'You busy tonight? We could go see that new Marvel movie.'

Joe laughs. 'I'm working. And I'm not eleven.' He pokes around in the drawer for a dry tea towel. Can't find one. Sits on the kitchen table to roll a cigarette. 'She's more Karen Gillan, Emma, I think. I'm sure I'm going to love her just the right amount.'

Wakes before dawn and hears the front door whisper. Up and to the window. The nurse is running east. Pulls on tracksuit and hoodie, laces Feiyue, greyly exits.

For a couple of blocks he trails her. He knows she is aware of him. That she is not afraid. This is foreplay.

When they get to the playground he hangs back. She is climbing up the fort—nimble, quick—to jump from the highest point. He feels himself tense as she pauses to centre before leaping off. But her landing is good, the roll smooth, rising up into a run. Does it again, and once again, ignoring him. The sky streaking black, orange and gold.

He watches for a time, moving on the spot—squats, stretches; a little walking on his hands—then goes to her.

'You've been practising.'

'You see how I'm landing? Protecting my spine? I can drop much further now.' Her eyes are bright.

'It's perfect.'

'It feels good.'

'Do you want to get higher?' He gestures vaguely towards the inky sky. 'I think you're ready.'

'Yeah.'

They run to his favourite laneway and he does a climb-up onto the wall, reaching down to her with his hand. She shuffles along the top on her bottom while he crawls cat balance, but once they hit the rooftops she finds her feet. He holds back so that he can watch her spring ahead. When she moves out of sight at one point he does a crane jump to a higher point, right foot hooked onto a chimney top, and there she is, a couple of houses away, in moving silhouette.

Back on the ground, they race, pulling up hard when they arrive at the bridge.

'You're fast, you know that?'

'You're faster.'

It's cold. He does a cat leap onto the side of the concrete platform under the northern end of the bridge and reaches down again. Pulls her up.

They huddle knees to chests, a metre between them, sizing each other up. 'Come here,' he says, reaching for her. She draws back. 'I know I fucked up,' he says. 'I hadn't been drunk in a long time.'

'I know. I mean it's obvious.'

'There's stuff I should maybe tell you.'

'No.' She looks at him so intently. 'I don't want you to tell me things.'

'So what *is* it that you want?'

'I want *you*.'

'And here I am.'

'But I can't have you.'

He frowns. 'The other night, that girl—it wasn't anything. You know it wasn't. I'm sorry. I wish I could take it back. But maybe it's time we made more of a commitment, give this a name.'

'Joe, do you think this could really work?'

'It does, doesn't it?' He reaches for her hands to try to warm them inside his. She lets him.

'We both know it can't last.'

'So you're going away. You could come back.'

She shakes her head. 'This—it's like the bridge. It carries us from one side to the other. And it's good, right?'

'I have a bridge. I don't need another one.'

'But that's all we've got. When I go I'm not coming back.'

He glares at her. What then is the point of all this? But he knew from the minute she walked into the house. This thing, this bridge, it is like one long erotic dream. He has always known that one day he will have to wake up. Sighs. 'Come here, with your struts and beams. I think you're missing a few screws.'

'Joe, that's a bad dad joke! A dirty dad joke.'

'I guess that makes you my long-suffering wife.'

He pulls her to standing on top of the platform, tucked away out of sight of the bike path and High Street, leaning up against the concrete vertical. Her fingers stroke the warm skin of his forearms; his trace the curve of her neck. They fumble with clothes, giggling, exposing only enough for it to be: economical; exquisite. In the cold pre-dawn. Outside of time.

After, she whispers in his ear, 'She wasn't right for you, that girl.'

'Fuck, now you're going to give me relationship advice? *Now?*'

'You need someone who will make your life complicated.'

'You could make it complicated.'

'Oh, Joe.'

'What. What?'

'Nothing. Just look up—the sky is beautiful.'

In bed on Wednesday the room is bright with morning sun. He is drinking coffee, wearing the old Bob Dylan t-shirt Todd offloaded. Really needs to go next door to do some washing.

Jack is up the corridor at the living room table working on his first law assignment and has been hurling complaints and facetious comments down the hall, both of them too lazy to move.

Joe opens the iPad, touches into Safari; looks up RMIT, Bachelor of Applied Science, phys ed.

It's a purely academic exercise. Ha. But his heart quickens as he navigates the page, reading carefully through each section. Like peeling wrappers off a present.

This program prepares you for a career as a specialist physical education teacher.

Coaching, health and fitness promotion and sport education for school- and community-based groups might be just some of your responsibilities.

You'll teach primary and secondary students in government and independent schools, and have the opportunity to teach students with disabilities.

'When did they drop the defence of provocation in Victoria?' The question ricochets down the corridor and takes a sharp right into his room.

'Why are you asking *me* that?'

Silence.

He reads about *global opportunities* and *pathways*, goes so far as *fees* and *entry requirements*. He lost his place in this course, stopped deferring, but he could reapply as a mature-aged student. Four years full-time. He could drop one of the jobs, use his savings. A fat HECS debt to work off. Be the dark horse at the back of the class who gets his essays in on time. He could do it. He knows he could. He could run it over.

Remembers looking at the brochures with Jen at the open day they attended on a Sunday in August of their final year. Drinking coffee in the Break 220 cafe, sharing pancakes, imagining themselves into new lives. She was going to do a straight Bachelor of Science at Melbourne. There was no question she would get the marks. He was going to study anatomy and biomechanics; he would take a bunch of kids and make them whirl.

By the time the offers came through she was dead.

All that's left on the page is *how to apply* and right there, at the brink, he steers away. And straight into Facebook. The solid weight of guilt, its unwieldy shape, is a corpse strapped to his back. It is the only definite thing, and he cannot put it down.

Hello.

Are you there?

Emily Dickinson is not.

He kicks off the covers and lies a moment longer, looking up at the ceiling. The spider is in hiding too. He imagines *being* the spider, and how fun it would be to run up the wall and across the ceiling. Could it be done? Not even if he spent the rest of his life trying.

14

'It's that spoken-word thing again with the great unwashed,' Lena announces as he pushes through the swinging door into the kitchen, hair wet from the shower.

He shrugs. 'So it will be slow.'

She is dusting sardines with flour; doesn't look up. 'They're starting early—something about a breastfeeding Iranian guest poet—and the fucking kitchen hand called in sick. Again. He's only been here, what, six weeks? And the dishwasher is broken. Fucking Boss. You know it's his niece's boyfriend?'

'I can help. Main bar's going to be quiet too. It's disgusting out there.' Gazing out the grimy window at the squall.

She stops to look. 'Godfather, it's been a long day. My cat got into another fight. I had to take him in a cab to the vet. I swear that animal is going to ruin me. Anyway, how are you?'

'I'm fine. Can't you give him cat bromide or something?'

'He's been desexed. He's just angry by nature.'

Joe laughs. Goes into the function room to set up.

Uses the broom to pull down cobwebs; lighting candles to cast uneven blue circles onto the rickety round tables; wiping away dust. Checks the audio equipment on the tiny corner stage, though it's not his job. Whose job is it? Then pauses, on his knees, when he hears Lena's voice. He is starting to know the salty sweet song. She sings it when she's stressed, to soothe herself. Never when he is in the room, but surely she must know that he listens.

He rocks back onto his heels; slowly rises. It's melancholic, her singing, and yet the quality of her voice: sort of twiggy and sun-shot, like her.

The bar staff arrive; frock up. Then it's time to unlock the doors, flick on the lights that sign: BAR NOBODY.

The event is well attended, given the rain. Probably down to the Iranian poet, who goes first. Moving through the room with loaves and fish, he catches snippets about a dying child and a shuttered window. The poet's own baby is at the back of the room, in the arms of a friend.

He retreats to the kitchen between orders to wash dishes. 'You've got a good voice, Lena.'

She is arranging leaves on white plates; floppy red nasturtiums circa 1980. 'You heard me?'

'Yeah, no, a bit. These are not soundproof walls.' Up to his elbows in soapy water.

'I was the lead singer in a band in high school.'

He turns to look at her, widening his eyes in a smile. 'Really? What did you do?'

'Rockabilly. We were going places, Joe. We represented the school at one of those Eisteddfod things.'

'Rockabilly? Ha. What, did you wear one of those flouncy skirts? A ponytail?'

'We all have our shady past, no?'

'I would have pegged you as a punk chick.'

He heads back out. And so it goes through the shift. The punters come and they go, like a slow migration of wildebeest.

Later, when the lights are off in the bar and they are finishing up in the kitchen before the cleaners arrive, 'The thing you were singing earlier, the thing you do, in Ukrainian.'

'It's a lullaby. "*Oi Khodyt Son Kolo Vikon*". "The Dream passes by the window, and Sleep by the fence . . . The Dream asks Sleep: Where should we rest tonight?"'

'It's nice.'

'My grandmother used to sing it. Now *she* had a good voice. Not anymore. Now she sounds like a poorly tuned radio.' She empties the remains of the limp salad mix into the bin. 'How's it going with the girl then, son of a carp?'

'She's going away. Some big trip she's planned.' Strange to say this aloud—Lena is the only one who even knows.

'And that's it?'

She's wearing one of her nauseating headscarves, swirls of gold and pink, pinned to her new short hair. It is coming adrift. He has a powerful urge to fix it.

'Apparently.' He starts counting their tips.

'I've been seeing someone too,' she says, after a bit.

He looks up, leans back against the wall with his arms crossed. 'Yeah?'

She is looking back at him. 'A boy I met at a gig. An electrician. Good with his hands.'

'Now there's a cliché.'

'Don't worry, Joe, I'm sure you're good with your hands too.'

He scowls. And she laughs, looks delighted. So he pockets his tips and pushes hers across the stainless-steel counter. 'For the cat.'

Pushes out of the kitchen, the heavy door swinging back and forth on its hinges between them, like an echo of their conversation—which he doesn't quite understand.

At Tiger Bridge she is confronted by the laminated sign pinned to a sandwich board: *7/8/14 Enclosure closed for repairs. We apologise for any inconvenience.*

'Oh shit,' muttered aloud, and in spite of the two young women who have pulled up beside her with their children. They'll think she's nuts, but, like, whatever.

'Where's the tiger, Mummy?'

'There is no tiger today.'

'But I want to see the tiger!'

'I know, darling. But they have to fix some things inside the tiger's house.'

'Why?'

'I know, why don't we go and see the orangutans!'

Elise proceeds over the tiny bridge alone to drop down onto the bench in front of the empty cage. What repairs? The enclosure is lifeless. She grits her teeth. She'd been counting on this. Tomorrow is Jennifer's birthday. She would have been twenty-two.

Elise called her Tiger Lily in preschool, so taken was Jennifer with the cats. She'd want to come here first and then last every visit, always twice. And the passion continued through childhood and beyond, in her drawings, t-shirts, books. For

Jennifer's sixteenth birthday she made her a cake with stripy icing. She always wondered if her daughter might not study zoology.

What was it with the tigers? she used to wonder. It seemed a generic choice for her wild curious daughter. But now she gets it. She just wasn't paying attention before.

'Happy birthday, honey,' she murmurs to the empty cage. Lets the tears stream down her face.

Anniversaries don't seem to be getting any easier. And there are so many: birthday; death-day; Christmas; Easter; Mother's Day; Halloween, with all those little trick-or-treaters—walking mnemonics; her own birthday, Adam's, Carl's. Endless associations. Though oddly, in the past couple of weeks, a building sense of anticipation—as if something wonderful is about to happen. As if she is about to deliver Jennifer all over again. She has been reliving her arrival, 5.32 am, how she barely made it to the birthing room before falling to her hands and knees. Adam interstate, catching an urgent flight back. The Irish midwife. She can almost feel the early contractions, even as she lucidly knows that tomorrow will come with no baby to hold, and that instead she herself will assume the foetal position.

She wanders over to the board that displays photos of the cats' faces and studies them for a while, cramming for her next round of spot-the-difference. Jennifer would have liked this game. No doubt she would have won. But there is no point in staying. She pours the dregs of her coffee onto the ground and walks out. There is always next week.

Cycles home and puts in a couple of hours on a leaflet for companion-animal veterinary products, then takes a long walk through the neighbourhood wearing dark glasses despite the dull sky. No one addresses her or seems to notice her go by. Is this how it would feel to be a ghost?

At twilight, she pours a glass of wine and perches on a stool beside the easel in the middle of the kitchen. She works on the figure in the background. Curled up, still in whites and greys and gentle folds of cloth, but with small splotches now of vivid red. The painting is nearly there, she thinks; it has taken on its own life—and imminent death. Soon she will start another. And then?

She and Adam have been speaking more on the phone; have started to ring one another of an evening, just to talk, in a strange disembodied way, about thoughts and feelings, the day they've had, like they did when they first met. He mentioned meeting again so she has started making bullet points on a piece of paper of all the things she wants to say. Meeting in person will require a more real and raw sort of conversation. But when she looks over the list now, sitting before the easel—on the night before the birthday—they all seem to say much the same thing: You were not there.

Why *was* she so stunned when he left? He was always halfway out the door. And yet she somehow still believed they were conjoined. He could pull away but at the end of the day neither would function without their shared lungs. The beating heart of the house. She was wrong—about them both.

And what might his bullet points include? Perhaps that she was there too much. Or maybe he is going to point out that, for all her being there, she was so often absent—somewhere away in her head. Her negligence, then, all the greater. How horribly and secretly have they come to blame one another?

She gets up and switches on background TV, pours another glass of wine, and prepares and eats a simple dinner of tuna and steamed vegetables.

The moon is large, lighting up the back lawn but also bleaching it of colour, like an old photograph. The wine has made her a little numb so she goes outside in her thin jumper and climbs the apricot tree. It's a perfect climbing tree, always was, with its solid, curving branches at just the right incline. Up, up, to where the children used to go. A perfect Y with a small bottom-shaped curve. They ate homemade icy poles up there in summer; retreated up there to sulk.

The curve is too small for her bottom but she wedges herself in at a slight angle and smokes a cigarette.

Jennifer was a cautious climber at first, unlike her gung-ho brother. It could take her twenty minutes to inch her way up the branch. Then, when she was too afraid to shimmy back down, Carl would parrot the golden rule: *if you can get yourself up, you can get yourself down again.* But then he was also the one who would go to her rescue, coming up behind to catch her fall, coaxing her backwards one shuffle at a time. She overtook him after that; became a fast, nimble climber with perfect balance. Though ultimately of course the rule was disproven, and Elise wonders pointlessly if things may have been different if she had not insisted so early on their courage and ragged independence, as if those sunny afternoons up in the canopy presaged the wreckage.

Elise coughs out a cloud of tobacco smoke and feels momentarily unbalanced, peering down at the sepia grass that grows on and on, year in year out, wordlessly regenerating. Resettles, and then lets herself start thinking about the next painting. They are strong climbers, those big stripy cats. She stretches out and up along the branch. Imagines a tiger in a tree: perhaps an apricot tree, implausibly; a limp body in its clutches.

When she finally goes back in she is feeling the cold, and her age. A scant few hours until Jennifer's birthday. She makes a hot-water bottle and takes it to bed with the iPad, to surf for tiger stories. Finds a new one. A man in a zoo in Jamshedpur who made his way through several security barriers to enter the enclosure of Raghav. Found unconscious but still breathing the following morning, his mental state under investigation.

She takes one of Adam's sleeping pills, and in the early hours she is cycling through a series of narrow wet streets that dissolve into a deep green jungle. Garlands of parasitic vines clinging to their slowly dying hosts, and the nervous chatter of monkeys and birds—so that she knows the tiger is near. She has to find her way back out so she can get to school pick-up. The bike is gone. She is running. But then she sees it, it leaps out from behind a tree, sudden and devastating, it is coming straight for her.

Wakes on the couch with her heart thumping, fists clenched, weeping for Jennifer. The truth made verdant and glorious: that life is fleeting.

—

The old man, sitting alone at his normal table, has a fresh bandage over one eye. Joe brings his coffee with the signature star, and a piece of cake. 'You been in a scrap?'

The man laughs. 'Cataracts, son. Price of growing old. They fix them up one at a time.'

'Does it hurt?'

'Not a bit.'

'Cake's on me.'

'Oh, no, there's no need for that.'

'Okay, it's on the boss then.'

'Very good of you.'

And back to the machine. Scooping in the rich dark granules; firing it up; one for the punter and one for himself, sans star.

He stands at the counter looking out onto the street, drinking his coffee. He's coming to like more the slow of the winter Sunday shift; that he's not run off his feet. He's already eaten two bowls of moussaka and been out on an errand to get a new needle for the record player, from some guy who works out of his garage in Preston. The sisters out back, cooking for the coming week.

Time whittles. He sweeps the floor and sluices the machine. Gives a little water to the cacti. Serves a middle-aged couple with matching iPads and tracksuits. Straightens the complimentary newspapers and puts on a new record. Retro-curls more butter to go with the date muffins.

And then free—to go and get Deck. A clear, dry afternoon. Running back along High Street, ducking behind the laundromat. The house is empty; the door of the lean-to pulled shut. He takes Sanjay's key from the nail in the kitchen and puts ten bucks into the car jar. Grabs the soccer ball and a bottle of water. Changes into a clean t-shirt and gets into the car, winds down all the windows so the cold air hits his face.

When he pulls up, Deck is waiting on the doorstep, hunched inside his hoodie. Arms crossed. Scowling beneath his curtain of hair. Joe is tempted to take a photo of him with his phone. Was Joe this transparent as a teenager? For sure, he was.

Deck ducks into the Citroen and slams the door hard. Joe whistles. They don't speak, not a word, until they've parked beside the oval at Coburg Lake.

Joe turns off the ignition, engages the handbrake. 'What's up?'

'*What's up?*' Deck mimics him.

Joe laughs.

So Deck punches the door. Lucky it is a shit-heap of a car.

'You were trying to be funny weren't you?'

Deck turns and gives him the full force of his glare; pure rage in his dark brown eyes. Something has gone down.

Joe looks right back; feels adrenaline shoot through his own system. Breathes. Blankly waits.

'I don't even like soccer,' Deck says at last, turning his back on Joe to look out the window at the park. 'Just take me fucking home.'

Joe doesn't say anything. Starts up the car again, reverses a few metres, pulls out.

They silently retrace their route. When they pull up, Deck looks at the unit then stares straight ahead through the windscreen for the count of about ten. Then gets out and slams the door hard. Again.

'Shit,' Joe mutters. He missed his moment; should have done something different. Winds down the window. 'You know where I am.'

Deck doesn't turn back.

'See you in a fortnight.'

You're trying to break up with me. Hands over her face, leaving only her green eyes exposed, all B-list starlet. *I can't believe this is happening.*

Jesus. Where do you even get that from? It's like we're having two different conversations.

I used to be enough for you. Why don't you just come out and say it? The last phrase amplified, as if he might not catch it.

Oh, for fuck's sake! He recalls that he hit his forehead with the heel of his hand in an outsized show of incredulity;

thinking, as he did, that she drove him to these dramatics. It was her jag—he wanted something easier.

In the corridor outside the chilly apartment. Facing off. The trance shit seeping out from under the door made him want to climb the walls. Not in a good way. A Saturday-night cocktail party at the ostentatious yet flimsy city abode of some friend of a friend of hers with family money. He didn't want to be there. That was it; that was all. She'd had a few drinks and was taking it personally. She always did.

You used to want to be with me. It didn't matter where we were.

Jen, I'm with you all the fucking time. *But now I want to go home. I'm tired. I hate these people. Why do you do this? It's sabotage. You should be having this argument with your father, not me. He's the one who's never around.*

Is it Kate? She's been calling you, hasn't she? She was laughing the other day about something you'd said.

No, no, no. He shook his head, clown-smiling. *Uh-uh, don't start. I'm not doing this anymore. I told you that.*

With the feeling of something constricting around his throat, he loved her less. In those final minutes he didn't love her at all.

But then, like an elite athlete, she drew on all her resources, managed to gather herself. *Okay. I'm not starting. Joe, see? I'm*

*steady. I just need you tonight. I do. Another hour and then
we'll go.*

The girl he loved. But he couldn't back down. There was
something at stake. He had no idea how big. Pushed open the
heavy door into the stairwell. *I'll call you tomorrow.*

He replays the conversation over and over. Nothing changes.

15

He is in Facebook and there it is: her birthday. Five days gone.

How?

Where was he?

A shift at the cafe and then, later, at the bar. He and Lena scratchy and the customer with angina. The ambulance—for the customers' viewing pleasure. But that morning, before dawn, he went playing with the nurse. That's what he did on Jen's birthday. He jumped around like a gibbon.

Joe?

—

You feel bad, don't you?
How did you guess?

I'm guessing you always feel bad when you come here.

I forgot her birthday.

Oh, Joe. It doesn't matter, it really doesn't.

It's the first time I've forgotten. How could I do that?

You don't help her, you know.

You don't say.

She would rather you did something with your life than just sit half in it.

What would you know about what she would want—or my life for that matter?

You're right.

He pauses to roll a cigarette; doesn't light it. Holds it in his mouth and types.

You know I'd left that night? I'd gone home.

I know.

So you were there?

I was with her at the end.

Fuck. He pulls on a coat and goes down the corridor, past the lean-to and out the back door; climbs the ladder onto the roof. Smokes the cigarette.

Comes back.

Joe? Are you there?

What do you want from me anyway Emily Dickinson?

I don't want anything from you. I'm sorry you feel bad. But Joe? There were a lot of people who felt responsible and me, I'm at the front of the queue.

Thursday, Joe and Sanjay are sitting at the kitchen table eating toast and no-brand peanut butter with chilli sauce. Emma is in the shower, and the nurse, the lean-to, dead to the world. It must be a lonely existence, hidden away from the light. He hopes that wherever she is going is worth it.

'You going to see Uncle today, bro?'

'Uh-huh.'

'May I join your noble self?'

'Of course. Emma?'

'No, big gig tonight. She has to practise.'

'I noticed there's been less screeching from the stereo lately . . . Her influence?'

'I will bring her around slowly. Song by song, there will be no rest until she sees the light.'

'No rest is right.'

Joe pulls on his beanie and waits out front while Sanjay gropes Emma goodbye. They set out to walk the nine blocks to the nursery.

'So, Brother Joe, here is the thing: she says she doesn't want children.'

'Interesting.'

'Mmm.'

'Well, she's only, what, twenty-one? You've been together about a week.'

'She says never—and it's good to breed young. You know, my guys, this is peak season.'

'Spare me, Sanjay. Jesus.' But he remembers those conversations—Jen's fantasy four.

'It's not just that. I love her, but sometimes I am the horse and she is riding me. No, not the Kama Sutra, Joey. She makes me run in circles.' And his long black hair, loose today, does shimmer like a well-groomed mane.

'She's smart. Is that a problem?'

'My father says I need to be a man.'

'Sanjay, you're a prince. Girls love you. You don't need to change.'

The prince sighs. 'So easy to be confused when you're talking to a fine woman.'

Now would be the time to tell his best friend about the secret crepuscular affair with its built-in use-by. But he doesn't.

They arrive at the nursery. Todd is in the kitchen-office, ledger open in front of him. The tabletop is dusty—no, it looks like it's smeared with horse shit. Probably is. Todd is holding one gnarled hand in the nest of the other, as if it is not quite part of him but a small animal, lame and tender.

'Boys! Grab yourselves a coffee. But first, you need to make it. And before that, I am hoping you might change the washer on the tap.'

'What a compelling offer.' Joe starts with the tap. There is no way Todd could manage this fiddly shit now. He opens the toolbox left conveniently on the bench, the packet from the hardware store; replaces the washer.

Sanjay pulls out a chair and sits down, fingering the new fronds on the chicken fern centrepiece. 'What jobs for us today, Uncle? Perhaps we could be starting with a brush and sweep?'

'Yes, yes, cleanliness is next to godliness, if you're Christian, which I'm not. Sanjay, I'm glad you are here too. I want you to be part of this. There is important business to discuss. I have good news!' Todd is pink in the face. Didn't have his post-lunch joint? 'There is fire blight to deal with and new seedlings to put out. But first! I have seen my doctor'—leans forward for the big announcement—'and I am planning to retire at the end of the year.' Leans back. 'What do you say?' Finishes by throwing his arms towards them, fingers deformed into permanent supplication. 'Can we keep the place open?'

Joe and Sanjay look at one another, Sanjay failing to conceal his pleasure. 'And this is good news?' Joe says slowly.

'Well, it could be—for you boys?'

'And how are you going to live?' he asks his uncle.

'I want to transfer half the business into your name, Joe, as my bequest. And Sanjay, if you can rustle up the funds, I want to sell the other half to you. The next part of this equation is that your mother could do with some financial assistance so I am going to put my apartment on the market and move into her place. I'm up for a disability allowance and I have something put aside.'

Joe whistles. 'Wouldn't you two drive each other insane after a day?'

Todd rumbles a laugh. 'We'll see.'

'It's not really part of my plan to run a nursery.'

'I thought you didn't like planning,' Todd reminds him. 'And Joe, what else are you doing, son? Pouring coffee? I want to do this for you. I know you could make a success of it.'

Joe looks back, unblinking.

And into this tension, Sanjay bounces out of his chair to start pacing. 'Uncle, I am deeply sorry for your pain. Frankly, life blows. But I am honoured by your proposal. To be a part of this garden of eden . . . if I can find the capital . . .'

Todd gestures to Sanjay to sit down. 'If it doesn't work out I'll put it on the market late spring. Joe, would you like to take a look at the books, get a feel for things?'

Joe receives the ledger reluctantly.

'We can talk again when you've had time to think. No rush, boys. Dream on it.'

'You've got to be kidding.'

He and the nurse are standing together on the ledge of the girder across from the pillar, in the hour before dawn. They are both dressed in black. A lone pigeon is cooing a protest at their presence—a watery futile refrain.

'At ground level I am doing fine. I'm not foolproof yet with the landing, getting it about eight times out of ten.'

'Eight out of ten? Joe. Don't you want to get it to a hundred out of a hundred?'

'Ideally, yes.'

She takes his left hand in her right, leans her head back against the ironwork and swivels to look at him. 'It's a long way down.'

'I thought you wanted to get up high.'

'I do.'

They hear a train in the distance. Her fingers squeeze his hard.

'Do you want to get off?' he asks.

'No, I want to stay for this.'

He loops a hand through a cheese-hole, gets a nice grip, and swings out over the drop gibbon-like, leaving one foot on the girder, so he can face her properly. 'So you think I can do it?'

She smiles. 'I know you can. But don't be rash, Joe. You're not Superman.'

'I know I'm not Superman. Why do you think I train so hard?'

She looks across again at the pillar. 'It would be incredible to see.'

'Promise I won't get wheeled in on your shift.'

'You better not.'

As the train rolls closer, her body grows rigid, pushing harder up against the girder, trying to flatten into it. He is worried she is going to bounce herself off; pulls himself back up onto the ledge to gently nudge her. 'It's okay. I'm right here.'

Seconds later the train roars overhead. The rush. The pummel. The triumph. She turns to him, beaming. 'We've come a long way, Joe.'

'We have?'

They sidle back along the girder and pounce onto solid ground. She springs away from him, does a passable run up the low wall, pulling up onto the concrete platform.

He cat leaps. Joins her.

She nestles into him. 'Easy shift last night but there was one guy . . . long-term user, came in with full-blown sepsis. Hands and feet swollen up like doughnuts. He'd been about a week before getting any treatment. He's going in for heart surgery today. I don't think he's going to make it. Maybe a few weeks, couple of months, but not long.'

'And?' Accustomed now to her patients and their critical conditions.

'He's young. Looked a little bit like you.'

'See my hands—just the right size.'

'I care about you, Joe. It's hard to say just how much.'

'Let's go back to the house and you can show me.'

'Catch me if you can.'

He lets her go, counts to twenty then sets off, levelling up about halfway home.

Down the corridor, tiptoeing; into the lean-to, with the window open and the river air flowing. Pulling at each other's clothes, not a sound. He kneels behind her on the floor, tracing the bridge of her body with his calloused hands. She pushes back against him. They can't get close enough.

Sprawled across her mattress, after, she tells him: 'We call it down time after an arrest, when they stop breathing. *You just have yourself a little down time, dear.*'

He laughs and shakes his head. 'You nurses and your gallows humour.'

'Yeah, we're a tough bunch, but we like them to go out easy if they can. It can be a cold hard place for some.'

Something in her voice pulls him up. He rolls over to look at her, searching, but she stares him down. There are places she will not go. She's said it again and again.

Closes her eyes.

'Sweet dreams, sick puppy,' he whispers.

And she mutters, eyes still closed, 'Just don't be too hasty with the jump, Joe. I want you to live.'

He stretches out on the mattress beside her to watch her fall off the world before creeping back to his room.

———

Elise leans out over the railing towards Hutan—she thinks—who is down at the water's edge surveying the gathered crowd. The kitsch orange-gold of a breaching koi complements his coat to perfection; you'd think the cat was about to start signing autographs. Aceh, glowing too with carnivorous good health, is busy sniffing, sniffing—the ground, the trees, the air; perhaps he smells spring coming? Or perhaps he smells

Elise, and wonders why the same dumb prey just comes back and back and back.

It's been a precious hour—still cold, but the place has been buzzing, human animals always so eager to quit hibernation. A little while ago, one guy said to another, overlooking the water: 'You could jump in, you know.' The other, clarifying: 'If you wanted to.' She loves that these interactions all worry at the same spot; the tigers hold their own.

And then, time's up. She finishes the last drops of her sweet coffee and shoves the empty cup into her satchel. Two answers short on the crossword so she refolds the sheet of newspaper and tucks it into the bag too. Buttons her coat and walks out.

She considered asking Adam to meet her here at the tigers but decided she wasn't ready, so they arranged a rendezvous in Fitzroy. It will be the first time they have been face to face in however long and she forgot her list of bloody bullet points. An act of sabotage or liberation—time will tell.

It's only after she has left the zoo premises, is riding her way bumpily towards him, that she feels the full weight of her trepidation. It takes all her willpower to stick to the course. She could send an apology text, claim a headache; keep talking to him on the phone under cover of dark. But Jennifer would say that was custard.

Peering through the darkened window of the pub, she sees him: alone at a table for two, against a wall without adornment, looking into the middle distance. She had expected sleek, compressed, professional, but seeing him there, clutching a pot of dark ale, he looks like a schoolboy playing truant.

She locks up the bike and stands outside for several minutes more, taking her time, smiling at an elderly passer-by who is weaving his way along the pavement in a state of blessed inebriation.

Goes in quietly; comes up from behind: an ambush. 'Hi.'

'Oh. Hello.' He stands abruptly and reaches for her out of habit or impulse. She offers a cheek. 'You're wearing that cinnamon stuff,' he says.

'Yes.'

She sits down on the chair opposite. Up close he looks more haggard—a man who has lost his grace. Not that she is bitter. 'You look well.'

He sniffs a laugh. 'No I don't. But you do.'

'It's the cigarettes and all-night parties.'

'Really?'

'Sort of.'

He smiles. 'I've been smoking too.'

'Duh.'

'I thought you didn't know.'

There is nothing to say to this.

'Do you want a drink?' he asks.

'Sure. What you're having.'

She watches him walk to the bar. He is wearing a navy suit. It fits him nicely. His black hair is spliced with grey. She remembers his naked body, wiry with all the schmoozing squash and lunchtime runs, skin with that soft papery quality of midlife but still the sun-drenched olive of his mother's Italian blood. She imagines—in a detached way—touching it, his flesh-and-blood, though it has been years since they visited one another with any real interest or passion.

He brings back her ale; puts it down in front of her. 'Lise.'

'Adam,' through gritted teeth. The use of her shortened name is presumptuous and infuriating but she bites it down.

An artificial log fire is radiating a somnolent heat into the stuffy room, all faux English cosiness. All that's missing is the sleeping hound.

Silence draws out, jarring with the comforting surrounds. He looks like he is struggling to find an opening statement, an appropriate emotion. She doesn't feel like helping.

'How are you?' he says eventually.

'Well, we spoke last night, remember? I'm okay. You?'

He nods slowly. 'You *are* okay, aren't you. Seeing you . . . I'm not. I've been wretched since I left.'

'You were wretched before you left too,' she points out and he grimaces. 'I'm sorry,' she adds.

'What for?'

'I'm sorry you're feeling bad.'

'I don't blame you.'

'No, well, you were the one who walked out.'

And what about how wretched she has been these past three years while he's gone off to work and kept functioning like a well-oiled tinman, avoiding getting too close in case he catches the grief?

'I know. And I'm sorry. You don't know how sorry I am. I made a mistake. I didn't know what else to do.'

She thinks this might be the first time he has ever apologised. Why doesn't it help?

'It's hard, isn't it, feeling things?'

'Yes.' He is calm but his eyes are bloodshot and imploring. So there is an old hound in here after all.

She sits on the edge of her chair. 'Adam, I don't think I'm ready for this. It can't be that easy, you know? You say sorry and we go home.'

'Lise, I don't even want it to be that easy. I hurt you and you have already been so hurt. I thought I could run away but it doesn't work like that, does it. You'd know that, seeing as you're the one with all the emotional intelligence.'

A girl approaches blithely with a pad. 'Are we having any lunch today?'

Adam: 'Can we have a bowl of chips?'

The girl raises plucked eyebrows and turns on her heel. This is, after all, a gastropub.

'I take it you're not ensconced in the new relationship then.' Elise digs her fingernail into the beer mat to make a geometric pattern.

'There is no new relationship. And that was never the point.'

'I don't even know if I care.' He grimaces again and she laughs. 'I haven't seen your face this expressive since those early days when we would sit and look into each other's eyes over our chocolate milkshakes.'

He smiles. 'Ugly, is it? Looking at me now?'

'No.'

'We never drank milkshakes. We drank cheap plonk.'

'Same thing.'

'Not exactly. We weren't naive. We were in love.'

'Or drunk.'

'How is your work?'

She thinks of the tigers, brilliant and alive, that hide behind the cover of her graphic design. 'Fine. There's enough.'

'I spoke to Carl yesterday.'

'Yes, I spoke to him last week.'

'He seems okay.'

She nods her assent. One child safe and accounted for.

Hand-cut chips arrive in a chunky white bowl with a pot of relish. Elise helps herself.

'I found someone we could go and talk to. She's supposed to be very good.' Adam looks at the fake fire. 'We need to talk about our girl. We haven't in a long time. And I know it's my fault.'

She looks at the fire too. The world hurts. She wipes her eyes with the back of her hand. 'I have been waiting so long, Adam, to share this with you. And now I'm just tired and angry. I'm sorry.' They are both so sorry.

'Can I make an appointment? It will be a wait.'

'I'll think about it.'

'Could we meet again soon? Coffee? Dinner?'

She doesn't respond.

'Lise, you can take all the time you need. I'm not going anywhere.'

She could slap him for saying this. Yet when she gets up to leave, she leans down and kisses him instead; a harsh sort of kiss, right on the lips.

16

Joe spends the weekend putting final touches on his mother's house. She hovers with a packet of shortbread and hands him orange segments with the pith removed, like he's four again. It's not a bad way to spend time with her really. The day is clear and cold and bright.

He is framing his old bedroom window in Wayward Wind and as he brushes away fresh cobweb and strokes down the muntin, meticulously avoiding the glass, he thinks that Jen would have liked the name and the colour: a pale blue-grey, not far from the late-winter sky.

It was what she loved about him that scared her, she told him once—his unruliness and dearth of fear. She had the last part wrong. He should have explained: he was always afraid.

In the late afternoon he finishes; walks the path to the front gate and turns to take it in. The house looks good: the Wayward Wind made sense of the Paperbark. His mother has donned oversized gloves and is doing some showy weeding of the barren bed that rims the lawn. Soon Todd will move in and bring the garden to life. Maybe it will even work out. They can be companionable curmudgeons.

He checks his phone again—a message from work and one from Sanjay with a picture of an overgrown parsnip wearing sunglasses. Clearly he has been busy with his many large responsibilities. Nothing from Deck. They were supposed to meet this weekend but Deck's mother called to say Deck was sick in bed and couldn't make it. He wonders if Deck is cutting loose—their agency agreement expired a long time ago—but it has come from nowhere. He has left messages but Deck won't pick up. It nags, and he misses him.

Presses lids back on tins, drops brushes into the jar of turps on the veranda for his mother to deal with. Heaves the enormous ladder back down the side of the house for the next time the roof leaks. Folds up drop sheets. Puts the paint tray in the laundry. Picks up dirty cups and cigarette butts.

What would Jen say to this industry from her all-seeing perch? She'd yawn. Hardly wayward. Hardly fearless. Another job done and still waiting for a pardon that can never come.

He has the night off so agrees to pizza shouted by his mother. She drives them to Carlton and they are guided into a woody interior by the first spruiker that hits on them. They never settled on a favourite taverna in all those years of coming here. It was always pot luck. A lot depended on the parking.

They order a large marinara pizza and salad. The green-and-white-checked tablecloth, the passata-perfumed air, floury cheese in a steel bowl, they all remind him of every other treat night. Birthdays, sporting victories; consolation after a trip to the dentist.

Her thin, greying hair tied back; hollowed cheeks; soft jowly chin. Her big olive eyes. He has tried so hard not to look at her or have her look at him these past few years, and while he was so busy not looking she went and shrank. He feels a wave of protective love—and remorse. Is this why he tells her he has been giving some more thought to university?

She almost chokes on her wine in an effort not to overreact. 'Oh.'

'I'm just thinking about it,' he reinforces.

She nods. And they hold one another's gaze—two powerful owls—and many things are rapidly said and done and then let go.

'Joe . . . your uncle. He is going to pressure you and your friend about the nursery. He can't help it.'

'I'm thinking about that too.'

'He loves you and he thinks he knows best. And it gives him something to cling on to.'

'I know.'

'I just don't want you to feel you have to do this for him if you don't want to.'

'Uh-huh.'

'Let me know if you want me to talk to him.'

He exhales loudly. 'We'll sort it out.'

'Yes, of course. Sorry.'

He leans back to rest his eyes on the ceiling. The plasterwork has a single deep fissure, jagged teeth running north-west. It's been poorly filled and touched up with a shade of pink that doesn't match the original. He used to look up like this when he was a kid and she was gazing at him too intensely, like she was going to swoop down and pick him up in her beak.

He forces himself to look back at her. His mother, who has always wanted the best for him. 'He didn't want you to know how bad it was getting,' he admits.

'Still my baby brother. His stubbornness hasn't helped. He's kept going too long with all the lifting and carrying. He hasn't looked after himself.'

They sit for a while without speaking, listening to the students flirting at the next table, the ceaseless traffic from the street and the humdrum background jazz.

'Joe, let's get gelati.'

'That's what you said when I failed my Year 11 maths exam—word for word.'

She smiles. 'Did I?'

'Yes. It was the perfect response.'

———

She has Carl and his girlfriend Maddy for Sunday dinner. They eat at the kitchen table with the easel tucked away in the laundry. She's lovely, the girlfriend. A kindergarten teacher, she has a dog, surfs, and does quilting in her spare time. Carl has pictures of her quilts on his phone. The patterns are primitive, colours earthy. You could hang them on the wall. Elise asks if she can order one; Maddy insists on washing up. This is going to be easy, Elise thinks, making tea, putting nuts and chocolate into a bowl. Not like when Jennifer first brought the boy home and Adam tossed and turned for a week.

Carl talks about his new job doing in-house IT support for a telecom. The pay and conditions are good and the work is fine. He has always worked to surf, and now he can hit the beach with his gorgeous girlfriend, looking up at the stars together by a sandy fire. Elise used to wonder how much her son's expediency was a reaction to his father's work ethic but she doesn't wonder anymore. There is no call for it. She thanks all the gods in heaven he is happy enough.

They don't mention the fact of the separation. They don't go in for anything too deep. But when her son goes to leave, he wraps her up in a big hug and she squeezes him back, feeling the manly weight of him. He feels like his father but his body also recalls his sister's—the particular way they both held themselves, so upright and game. So that in his arms she is embracing the both of them.

One day soon, when the time is right, she wants to tell him what a beautiful, patient brother he was. He always had Jennifer's back, even when she was riding him. But there is a present to inhabit so she hugs Maddy too and begs them to come back soon. 'I'll make it worth your while,' she jokes. 'I'll cook anything you want. Maybe I could pay you?'

She drags out the easel after they've left and spends a couple of hours on the tiger in the tree. The body in its arms looks dead but the cat clasps it as a lover might. The work is getting finer, compared to the first big-brush paintings. She is spending longer on them, and rather than moving on to the next when she can get no closer, she is reworking—rubbing back and repainting, trying out new backgrounds, experimenting with the light source. Trying to get to it, the elusive unnameable thing.

Her phone pings; she ignores it. Each day now, at a random hour, Adam sends a single message. It is like a measured dose of medicine for their marital disease. In tiny clusters of unpunctuated words she can see how he is trying to remind her of his attention to detail, his memory, his way with words and, above all, his love. It is like watching a tragedy in texts: the father of her children, whom she is no longer sure she wants, finally unwrapping his own sad, sharp present.

And then a message last week from Tom about catching up again, whatever that means.

She paints and smokes her readymade trash, and when she needs a break she fiddles on the iPad—looking for new stories, images; ways in. Though she misses newspapers and library reading rooms, the literal cut-and-paste, she does love the way this new technology enables every wild-goose chase.

———

When the bar has shut and they've cleaned up and changed, Boss comes in, all white teeth and aftershave. The staff meeting is a biannual imposition that he insists on staging late at night, when everyone is too fucked to talk back.

They go in his black Mustang to Gertrude Street, Lena in the front passenger seat, Joe and the niece's boyfriend in the back. Boss plays Ryan Adams's *Heartbreaker* and Lena and Joe smile at one another. The rest of the staff make their own way there. Twelve in all show, including the super-casuals who work a shift a month but can't seem to fall off the roster completely.

Another dark grimy bar much like their own. Boss orders a few jugs of beer; anything else is on them. Joe drinks tap water. They work through customer complaints, the chronic lateness of one of the bar girls (who hasn't actually turned up for the meeting), staff requirements for upcoming events, the prospect of a very minor renovation, and the question of who has been leaving such a mess of hair in the shower.

Joe sits at the opposite end of the table to Lena and they endure the tedium through an elaborate nonverbal conversation. At one point Lena engages in a mime of scratching that Joe guesses relates to the niece's boyfriend's dreadlocks, or perhaps is suggesting Boss is a monkey. Then Lena drags the meeting out by making a few complaints of her own, which the rest of them support in theory but not in practice given it is nearly four in the morning. Clever Boss.

After the meeting's been closed, Boss takes off, a few of the staff stay on to drink, and Joe offers to walk Lena home. It's been a long time since they've left work together.

'It could have been worse,' he comments as they walk north-east towards her apartment.

'How so?'

'He might have tried a team-building exercise again, like the one with the grapefruit. After he'd done the manager's training course, remember?'

'True. But you know, Joe, I'm at the end of my tether with this job.'

'You're kidding.' Droll.

'I'm thinking of moving on.'

'Aren't you always?'

'Would you miss me?'

They turn a corner. 'You know I would. You're the best thing about that place.'

He looks at her and she grins under the streetlight. 'He's not a bad man, Boss, but he's sure as hell not a good one.'

'Show me a good man, Lena.'

'You, Joe. You're a good man.'

He laughs, and shoves her sideways.

'Want a cup of tea?' They are at her apartment block. He's never been inside.

'Have you got beer?'

'I thought you didn't drink.'

'Keep up, Lena.'

Two flights up the external staircase. Over the threshold and into her domain. She switches on a standing lamp that softly illuminates the snug space. There is lots of blue and slashes of red—pictures, objects, fabric; wooden blinds. He perches on the edge of a worn blue leather armchair and the infamous tomcat comes and wraps himself around Joe's legs.

'What's his name again?'

'Carver.'

'Living up to it then.'

Lena opens beers and he rolls two cigarettes, passing her one. They sit companionably and watch the late, late movie, a Ginger Rogers and Fred Astaire. Carver curls up on Joe's lap. He looks up once to find Lena smiling at him and he smiles back and it is disquieting, the way he feels it in his body. You can be friends with a girl, right?

Doesn't leave until almost dawn then runs straight to the bridge, in his peripheral vision the shapes of the trees and shrubs more animal than vegetable. Gazes down the underside of the bridge at the pillar. He knows it is too soon to jump, but it's so close now he can taste it, like the beer and cigarettes.

Warms up for a while. Does some pole hops, swapping one forefoot for the other, swiftly, back and forth, atop a post. Then some *quadrupedie*, cat-light on the metal steps. He is wearing the wrong shoes but he wets the soles and does a few wall runs. So easy now to reach those six bolts.

Keeps looking back over his shoulder at the pillar. All stirred up.

Fuck it. He climbs up onto the girder and sidles along until he is facing one of the nearer pillars. He is glad the nurse is not with him. He could take a calculated risk. He hasn't had much to drink. A dress rehearsal of the real thing: if he doesn't make it he'll only drop twelve feet onto concrete. He could do that in his sleep.

He stands in neutral for a long time, spine perfectly erect, toes hanging over the edge: feels his heart hasten—he's been training for this for months, for years, for all his fucking life—and then uses that same training to slow the race down.

Draws on everything he has learnt to date. Is his thinking clear? Are his motivations correct? Never. So that after a motionless, timeless wait he then springs without warning, without countdown: a huge, controlled leap, like a cat, all according to plan, lower body overtaking upper mid-jump, feet landing softly, but too low, on the wall. Only one hand catching the top of the pillar, and, knowing the move is lost, letting go, dropping vertically down, all nice and soft for landing but for the slight incline on the surface he hadn't factored, because he didn't fucking prepare, so that his right ankle twists sharply as his body folds. Rolls sideways a few times, the impact of the drop running over and out.

On his back, probing the ankle with his hand. It hurts but it's not broken. He would like to use it to kick himself. What was he thinking? You never play when you've been drinking and up all night. You don't try something new. Wrong shoes. Wrong intentions. Of all the stupid fucking things.

He lies there for a while swearing then limps slowly home, stopping at the 7-Eleven for tobacco and milk. Gets an icepack out of the freezer and goes to bed, his ankle already starting to swell.

Tries Deck again before he goes to sleep. He wants to wake him up. No answer.

17

Chocolate fairy bread is new on the menu—for mothers of preschoolers to order gratefully then loudly deride. *I never give him sugar at home!* He slathers the sliced sourdough with the organic chocolate spread, sprinkles hundreds-and-thousands. Does it quickly. Makes a mess. Wipes up.

Peak hour on a Thursday, the cramped cafe is in perpetual motion. Mothers with their offspring move in and out, up and down, with toys and tissues and spills and embraces, as if they've been wound up and are mechanically releasing. Workers wanting takeaways. *Make the coffee hot, yeah?* Students. Misfits. Both sisters out front and all three of them hard at it, responding to every dumb-arse preference and particularity as if it were only common sense. The old man taking his sweet time with his coffee and cake, savouring the hullabaloo with his one good–one rheumy pair of eyes.

Joe tries to ignore the phone but it keeps vibrating in his back pocket. On the fourth call he picks up mid-order, holding it to his ear with his shoulder while he steams milk.

It's Deck's mother, Marie. He puts the stainless-steel jug down, stands back from the coffee machine.

'I hope you don't mind me calling, love.'

'Not at all. Is everything okay?'

'It's all good, I was just wondering if you've heard from Deck?'

'No . . .' He has a swooping sensation in his gut, like he has missed the last train home.

'He had a little disagreement with Frank and he's taken off.'

'You don't know where he's headed?' He recalls the man's face, peering through the window at Deck's birthday. Frank was the reason Deck took off last time. At least Joe never had to deal with a stepfather.

'That's it. He's not at school—I spoke to his teacher. You know what he's like. The mouth on him!' A high, false note meant to reassure them both.

Voula is giving him the evil eye. He'll become impotent or only sire piglets. 'He's probably walking it off,' Joe says, picking up the jug again to finish steaming the milk, phone to shoulder.

'He's been a right little monster lately. And this morning . . . they had a tiff, nothing major. It got a bit heated. They both said things they didn't mean.'

'He'll cool down.' But his skin is crawling and he doesn't want to talk to her anymore. He wants to talk to Deck. 'I have to go, Marie, or I'm going to get fired. Sorry. I'll call you if I hear anything.'

He hands the takeaway flat white to the wanker from the wine shop next door. The wanker puts five cents in the tip jar.

'If you speak to him, Joe, could you tell him to come home? Tell him his mother loves him.' Another laugh, like something being squeezed. 'He listens to you.'

'No he doesn't,' he says. 'We'll talk later.'

During the next infinitesimal lull, when the sisters' backs are turned, he tries Deck's phone. No answer. Sends a text: *Are you ok? Call me.* Marie has to be worried if she's ringing that metropolis of a school. He should have gone over last Sunday and seen him face to face. He knew something was up. Deck the monster doesn't scare him.

Lunchtime comes and goes through a king tide of lentil soup, moussaka and chicken sandwiches. The fairy bread sells out so he makes more, arranging it on the ornate silver tray with a cascade of strawberries; sliding the whole into the polished display case. Washes load after load of dishes.

Keeps checking his phone. Sends another text. If he knew where to go he would go there. If he knew where to start looking.

—

The thing about the tigers is that they remain.

If she kept coming, week in and week out, year after year, might she one day earn herself a tiger greeting—the ch-ch-ch they reserve for one another and favoured keepers, a signal of trust and affection? She shudders at the conceit of this daydream, to want such a thing when she has already gleaned so much.

Lately she has been playing sound clips of wild tigers in bed at night, tracks she finds on the internet: the deep territorial rumble; gentle chuffing between mothers and babies, between siblings; the exhilarating roar of an ambushing cat. There is something about closing her eyes and listening that brings the tigers ever closer, till she can feel them in the room, their hot rank breath, pacing the perimeter of her bed.

And by day she has been reading up on tiger tourism in India, the pros and the cons. Clearly it is a gross invasion to wade into tiger territory on elephant-back with your SLR, but they make a case in favour, too: how profits go towards conservation and give the villagers an economic incentive to keep the cats alive. And to go there, to really go there, to the heart of the jungle: it was a dream of her daughter's that has somehow become her own.

No jungle to speak of here at Melbourne Zoo but Indrah is in a state of repose in front of the stand of bamboo. Elise has brought her sketchbook along for the first time and when she's finished her coffee she sets up the portable easel she picked up with the last pay cheque. A carbon indulgence, it folds down to nothing, flicks open like a switchblade, and then manages to be as sturdy as the real thing.

She gets a few curious looks as she sets up but they soon move on. A middle-aged woman with a hobby, bully for her. Opens the sketchbook to the working page and rests it on the easel; takes out the battered tin and, from within, the chewed stub of a favourite charcoal pencil.

Her most recent painting is finished and she is moving towards something new. She wants to explore and challenge her sense of the tiger's proportions. Those enormous forepaws with which the tiger rides the prey into the ground, the hefty hind legs used to stabilise, and for leverage. She wants to understand how it all works.

A zookeeper she recognises wanders by carrying a bucket and a clipboard. 'Come on, draw me!' he hollers. 'I'm cuter.'

'Keep still, then.'

'If only I could.'

She laughs. She still hasn't told anyone but Jill about this thing that occupies most of her sleeping and waking thoughts. And the young zookeeper is her intimate without knowing or caring. Perhaps her clockwork attendance is nothing special; maybe there are others who take up their places around the zoo at different times on different days, holding their own private vigils.

She draws loosely for now, sweeping curves and lines, because this is about dynamics, interior relationships. Indrah knows she is being measured and quartered but doesn't seem to mind, closing her eyes for long seconds at a time. What does she dream of? Her mother Binjai, stuck up in the godawful little cage between the cheetahs and ocelots? Her brothers, whom she can smell and hear but never see? A troupe of dancing gazelles? Mmmm.

Elise reaches inward too, losing her senses, so that it's well after twelve before she surfaces with a bunch of sketches half seen, half imagined. And then a moment of panic at overstaying, as if all this is going to turn to dust. She packs up, heads out, wearing her light plaid jacket now the earth is beginning to stir. Has to get back to start a new job—a 1-2-3 local government brochure pack on accessing services for mothers to be, of all things.

Buys sushi on the way home, then works all afternoon at the kitchen table, fitting in a freebie for Jill. At five she heads out for a walk. Along the same streets she's always walked; past the same houses with their changing facades and new storeys. The house on stilts she once coveted, nicknamed the Stork, with its huge peppermint gum out front and the broken children's swing; the sixties orange-brick units with their communal orchard of fruit trees.

She remembers carting the children around these streets in a double pusher, bags of shopping hung from both handles in a vain attempt at balance, an umbrella lodged between them for shelter from the sun and rain. She would stop at the greengrocer, where everything was limp and overpriced; buy handmade sausages from the butcher. A coffee at the Italian bar where there was always a table of old men playing cards. She was never welcomed there but she liked the dark, slightly taut ambience, and with time the children wore those men down. While they remained reserved with her they took to pinching her babies' cheeks, giving them sweets and bottles of apricot nectar. The children would start squirming as soon as she turned the corner into the tiny shopping strip, yearning towards the den of iniquity.

Or she would walk further still to the municipal library for a stack of picture books and a novel that required little concentration. Or to the home of an old family friend in the next suburb, a single lady in her seventies—nineties, now—who liked nothing more than to chitchat about the young things on the corner dealing drugs and the pains in her legs. The woman brewed a strong tea served in cup and saucer, and Elise would leave that house feeling pleasantly trodden on, ready to drink in the fresh air and slobber kisses onto her children's warm rosy skin.

On her weariest days, she wouldn't get out at all. Carl would run around the house and garden wielding a stick at imaginary foes. Jennifer plonked on a blanket somewhere, kicking fat legs in the air, or later with her tin of beads or drawing paper. Or the two little cherubs up up up in that tree and Elise flat on her back on the grass, gazing up at the blue sky, hollow with fatigue, boredom and despair. Early motherhood was cloven—desperate one hour and rapturous the next. You never knew on waking what lucky dip of hours lay ahead.

And yet walking the streets now, it is those early, relentless days she longs for the most. The days counted in hours. Her heart aches for each and every one of them.

Returning at dusk to the empty house, she runs a bath. Pours wine into the last-standing tulip—a wedding present— and puts on Billie Holiday. Slides into the water, closes her eyes and thinks about the tigers that once ranged all the way from Turkey to Russia. Imagines a world where the tigers come back, rebuilding territories on the wreckage of human civilisation.

Wakes some time later in cool water and silence. Adam used to hate this falling-asleep-in-the-bath thing but he is not here, and she still is.

———

Early evening, after speaking twice more to Marie and a useless conversation with a desk sergeant, a message from Jack: *Your urchin is on our doorstep smoking your tobacco.*

He texts back: *Coming.*

'Okay if I leave a bit early?' he asks Georgie. Almost closing and he's worked a double shift, the crowd thinned now to after-schoolers drinking coffee and talking big, both of which will keep them awake.

'Of course. You never ask, honey. Everything okay?'

'Friend in need.'

'Your friend okay?'

He shrugs.

She fills him a sack of biscuits and slaps his arse as he heads out.

Runs all the way home, past the tobacconist and tattooist, the curtain shop and the gun shop. He is still limping slightly on his bandaged ankle but the ligaments were overextended, not torn. He's been doing heat, ice, stretching, resting—now he has to get back to where he was.

When he reaches the laundromat and rounds the corner, sees Deck on the front doorstep wearing one of those silky American baseball jackets, he could cry with relief.

Pulls himself together. 'What's with the horrible jacket?'

'You wouldn't understand. You're too old.' Deck is hunched up like a rhesus monkey though the weather is mild.

Jack, bespectacled at the open doorway, enjoying the drama. 'I just found him out here. He didn't want to come in.'

'Can't believe you live behind a laundry, man.' Deck shakes his head in wonderment.

Jack returns to the living room and his books. Joe limps down the corridor and into the kitchen. Deck limps after him.

'Are you making fun of my injury?' Joe asks.

'No, I think I broke my toe when I kicked the wall.'

Joe laughs. 'I fell off a pillar.' Finding the pliers, turning on the stove; filling the stained espresso maker. 'Coffee?'

'Yeah.'

'So what did you get for kicking the wall?'

Deck lifts his chin up to disclose the choker of red marks around his throat. Sheepish. 'I asked for it. I broke his favourite mug, too.'

'So he tried to choke you?'

'Said he was going to kill me. Fucking thought he was, too.'

'I'm going to go and break his favourite bowl.'

'I'm not going back.'

Joe nods slowly.

'He hates me. Everything I say he's like, *Mummy, Mummy*, making fun of me and then if I talk back he smacks me. He told my mum maybe it's not too late for an abortion.'

'He's a fucking arsehole.'

'He lost his job so lately he hates me more.' Deck is shivering.

'Where have you been all day? The alps?'

'Northland. I got new hi-tops. See? And I watched that ball thing, you know, the giant marble run?'

Joe ignores the stolen goods. 'Yeah, up by the cinema.'

'I watched it for hours, man.'

Joe rummages in the cupboard and fridge, remembers the biscuits; puts them in front of Deck. Deck takes one out of the bag, examines it, and then eats it slowly, as if it is important now not to show hunger or weakness of any kind.

Joe sits down opposite him. Fuck knows what they are meant to do.

'I'm not going back into the system.'

'You can stay here. We'll work something out.'

Deck chokes back a sob then, like there is still a pair of hands around his throat. Joe reaches over and rests a hand on Deck's shoulder until he shrugs it off.

'By the way, I do like soccer.' Deck's red eyes smirk an apology through the curtain of hair.

'Duh. I know that.'

'I don't want to speak to my mum.'

'I already texted. I'll call her later. What about your dad? You want to speak to him?'

'What's he going to do?' Deck snorts. 'Throw me a line?' But his desire couldn't be clearer if it was tattooed across his neck, like the bruises.

'I don't know. Maybe. You were going up to see him in a few weeks anyway, right? For term break?'

So Deck gets out his phone and calls his dad, going out the front into early evening to talk.

Joe sits at the table and wonders what his own dad would do. He can't remember when he last spoke to him. Several Christmases ago at least.

Deck comes back in and slouches into the chair, visibly more relaxed. 'Yeah, so I'm going up there. I have to get a bus. He said can you lend me some money for the ticket and he'll send it to you?'

'I'll drive you in the morning. Why not? I've got the day off. You can sleep on the couch.'

'What about school.' It is statement not question.

'Maybe you could organise for the school to send you some work. You're smart. You'll keep up.'

Deck nods, drums his fingers on the tabletop.

'You still hungry?'

'A bit.'

They walk up the street and get a parcel of fish and chips then share them with Jack in front of *Law and Order*, which Jack critiques with great earnestness. Then Deck asks Jack about shoplifting laws and Jack makes shit up on the spot. Enjoying the audience, Jack offers the delinquent a beer—which Joe vetoes—and admires his new hi-tops.

Joe ices his ankle and looks on. Enjoying, like a chemical high, the sight of Deck in his living room, safe.

'That one's all right,' Deck says to Joe when Jack's gone to bed. They're still up, watching an American talk show. 'The other one's weird. The one with the long hair.'

'He grows on you,' Joe explains.

So we meet again.

Hardly.

You wouldn't want to—not really.

Three heads or four?

Five, and claws.

Sounds exciting.

Hardly.

What have you got for me today then, Emily Dickinson?

What do you miss about her most?

Oh you make this difficult.

Just one thing then—anything.

He tosses the iPad aside and lifts his body into an inverted bridge. Holds it. Releases.

I miss how she made everything into an adventure even if it was just going to the dentist. Sometimes it was exhausting but I miss it.

Yes! I miss that too.

What about you, what do you miss?

I miss the way she would challenge me.

Yes she was definitely challenging. You hide in here asking these questions, Emily. Are you happy?

Sometimes. Isn't that all you can ask for, Joe?

I didn't know you could ask. Who you asking?

LEAP

Today was a good day.
Yeah, my day was good too.
See—that makes me happy!
Why?
To be honest, I don't exactly know.
You don't, do you.
Ha.

18

When he gets back from the eight-hour drive, after a late start, an hour in Lakes Entrance and food stops, it is almost midnight. There is a low glow in the window of the lean-to. Must be the nurse's night off.

Jack is finishing an essay at the living-room table, more head-bent than hell-bent these last days of winter. Joe says goodnight then creeps past unseen to the back of the house, to the golden seam of light beneath the door. Gently pushes it open.

She is lying in bed with *Mosby's* splayed across her chest, the lamp burning. Without a word he takes off his clothes. She watches, smiling. Slides in next to her. Drinks in her perfume of trees and water.

'I wish . . .' she whispers. Doesn't finish, and they lie side by side listening to a possum growling in the backyard.

She switches the lamp off and laces her fingers through his.

Head spinning with the road and the lights, too much coffee and the image of Deck perched on the edge of his dad's couch, grinning. 'I wish too,' he says finally.

'It's getting harder to see each other, huh?'

'We live in different time zones.'

'Maybe it's good. Like a weaning process.'

'Is that what this is?'

'This doesn't have a name.'

She slides her hand down his chest, over his stomach. And he turns to look into her big felid green eyes, lit up by the moon. 'Do you believe in ghosts?' he asks her.

He is with Jen; they are squished into his single bed, whispering in the dark.

She doesn't answer. Puts fingers over his lips, caresses him.

He moans; runs his hands sleepily over her breasts, the bones of her hips, reaching between her legs. She quickens to his touch and they are barely human anymore, all nerve; nothing matters but this. 'Do they all want you? All your patients?'

'Well, most of them can't even see me. They're unconscious.'

Her words bring him back. He sits up, turns on the lamp. 'I can see you.'

She sits up too; facing him. 'Yes.'

Hands running lightly over skin like some sort of ancient ritual where every square inch has to be blessed. She makes circles on his chest; he strokes the wings of her shoulder blades. And as he is touching her, what he sees is her leaping across rooftops like a cat, swift and impossibly sure-footed.

'You've changed things for me,' he whispers.

'I know.' She smiles. 'That was the plan.'

'You had a plan? This is cracked,' he mutters, and suddenly there are tears sliding down his face; hot, wet, they fall onto her cool skin. 'Everything about this is cracked.'

'Like the universe.'

'Yeah, and the footpath.'

'Time.'

'Sex.'

'Like love.'

Later, lying in one another's arms in the stark moonlit cell, she tells him she has booked her ticket. He doesn't even ask when she is leaving.

JUMPING

19

Joe rearranges shifts at the cafe so he and Sanjay can help Todd every Saturday—behind the scenes, leaving his uncle to serve. In his reduced capacity, Todd appears smaller to Joe, like he is being returned to himself, this century-old fern. His hands are the dying fronds.

'So I've looked at the books,' Joe says at smoko. 'Looks shit—but then you already knew that.'

Todd waves this away. 'With two able-bodied young men, business will pick up. The sky is the limit.'

Joe sighs. 'You have magic beans?'

And then his uncle and Sanjay are off, talking up a leaf-shaped sandpit down the back for toddlers, surrounded by herbs to pluck and sniff. Sanjay wants a wire igloo with a small gaggle of chooks and a stand of tube plants indigenous to the local area. Todd and Sanjay moan about the overused 'native', denoting such a vast and broken family. The tubes could be by the checkout and cheap enough to buy with loose change, like candy at the supermarket. And how cool it would be, Sanjay's eyes wide, to hold workshops on caring for your carnivorous plant and how to transform your nature strip.

Joe offers, 'I could put a frothy star on top of *everything*.'

'Yes!' Sanjay enthuses. 'A coffee machine! We'll have tree stumps for people to sit on. They'll come just for your coffee, Joey, you know they will.'

But try as he might, none of it makes his heart race.

Whenever he can he has been going to the bridge to train—alone. The taciturn spring mornings are sublime, when the city is still half asleep but there is a sense of nascent life, in the trees, on the ground, in the rippling brown creek. Repetition after repetition, he is rebuilding and conditioning. Testing the outer limits of his body and how it intersects with the environment; every edge and surface and gaping space. He would like to understand these dynamics so well that he cannot ever again be blindsided, even as he knows this to be a dream. Apparently, he is not Superman.

He has been working the cat leap onto the side of the concrete platform. Working it. Working. Getting the move seamless somewhere in the vicinity of nineteen out of twenty. And each time, he finishes the session by edging along the girder to the very centre, right up high. Spending time in posi-tion, motionless: assessing, imagining; normalising; preparing. He knows every detail of this structure now. There will be no surprises.

She believed in him, Jen. It's the part he'd forgotten. Not just a delinquent fuckwit but someone worth loving.

Tom suggests a drive to see the first spring blossom; up into the hills, visiting a few of those private gardens. He'll make a picnic and could she bring cushions? And now it is Sunday morning and Elise is taking a look at herself in the mirror—really looking.

Sees: a woman of small proportions and slightly less-than-average height; iron-straight black hair to her shoulders, short fringe; milky white skin that cannot tolerate too much light; green eyes, large for her face; the hint of an overbite; and the pull of gravity on all of this. A woman who once hitched a ride on her looks and has now moved neatly into reverse. Ha. Her people are not long-livers—maybe one great-great-grandfather who made a hundred—and she is sure she has passed some sort of halfway mark. There should have been a bugle.

Also, she sees that with the swimming and walking she is still strong—even a little mean. And that her hands, though threaded with hairlines, are still fine; her favourite body part, tools and playthings, with crescents of paint under the nails. And her eyes, so like her daughter's, have not changed much. They can still distract.

She doesn't spend a lot of time looking in the mirror but here it is: the vanity of youth only grows with youth's passing. She should have enjoyed it more while she could, as with everything.

Pulls on black jeans and cherry-red lace-up boots. A grey wool jumper; light blue cotton scarf. Finishes her coffee and drags the easel into the laundry just in case Tom comes inside.

Does she want Tom to come inside? This invitation to pick daisies, the suggestion of cushions and wine, no wonder she is edgy. She can see how Adam's departure may have opened a door that has always been slightly ajar. And here she is at the mirror again, straightening her eyebrows with a thumb. Does this mean she cares?

Ready early, she washes dishes, puts stewed apples into a tub, chucks out some takeaway curry. And there at the back of the refrigerator shelf is the sourdough starter, left for dead. She takes it out.

She brought this wild thing to life over twenty years ago, watching it ferment like an expectant mother. Kneading the dough helped her ride out the tumult of family life. When they went on holiday, Jill would babysit the acrid life form, feeding and watching over it. Then when Jennifer died it was all she could do to keep the thing going, it demanded so much flour and water and attention. She did; she persevered. It was an act of faith and diligence. But since Adam walked out she has not fed the thing once. She has been trying so hard to remember what the point of all this was. Your heart gets smashed to bits. Love is hell. You can buy bread at the shop.

She takes a spoon out of the drawer and pokes at it. Recalls the sour-fresh smell that filled the house with the weekly baking, how Carl and Jennifer ate the bread warm with jam and butter, and Adam turned it into toast with scrambled eggs. She peels back the thick carpet of black gunk with its disconcerting flower of crimson, and chucks it into the compost. Gets a clean bowl and salvages a couple of creamy spoonfuls from the very bottom of the jar. Adds flour and water, stirs, and yes, almost instantly, first bubbles rise to the surface. Life persists.

Sets it on the bench to warm up and covers it with a tea towel. Texts Adam: *Where did you get that last sack of flour from?*

And then the brass knocker and Tom at the door, good as new.

———

The batteries in the Bollywood door chime are almost flat but no one is going to change them till it dies completely. This is a given. What was overwrought has become disturbing, like a badly recorded soundtrack of torture in the depths of the jungle.

'Can someone answer the fucking door!' Jack shouts from the living room.

'You get it, you lazy pangolin!' Sanjay shouts back from his room.

Joe rises from his bed, where he is reading about student loans on the iPad, and strides up the corridor. 'You owe me,' he calls to them both, 'and one day I am going to cash it all in.' He does a quick systems check as he moves and his ankle feels good. Time to lose the bandage.

It's Emma. They do their do-si-do and then she goes into Sanjay's room and the door closes.

Joe heads to the kitchen, finds the pliers, empties baked beans into a pan.

There are raised voices from Sanjay's room and Jack comes into the kitchen, smirking. 'Trouble in paradise.' He adds a second tin of beans to the pan so Joe hands him the wooden spoon and puts his foot up on the table, pulls off the elastic bandage, stretches.

Minutes later the front door slams and they hear Sanjay cursing and kicking the broken skirting board in the corridor. After a while he comes into the kitchen, takes his shortbread tin out of the cupboard and sits at the table to silently unpack a foil and his papers; rolls a number. Once he's lit up, 'She says I'm self-absorbed because I didn't call her yesterday when I knew she was feeling sad.'

Jack tuts and takes the joint out of Sanjay's hand. Joe pours beans into bowls.

'She came to pick up her violin,' Sanjay continues. 'But she said she wants an adjournment—no, that's not it, a . . .'

'Whatever.'

'. . . *sabbatical*, that's what she said. She's having doubts about our compatibility. And she says I'm too carefree, like it's a bad thing.'

'She's just pissed off,' Joe says. 'Give her a couple of days.'

'Yeah, no, last week she was talking about a Hindi wedding in the bush with her musician friends and strings of paper lanterns. Can you *see* my mother?'

They all chuckle.

'You'd probably start a bushfire,' Joe notes.

'She's high maintenance.' Jack is sage. 'You should have your own sabbatical. We'll go to town. Make the ladies swoon.'

'Don't listen to him; he's just jealous,' says Joe.

'And you're not, lover boy? Don't see you getting much.'

Joe pushes his empty bowl away. 'She'll be back, Sanjay. You two will be fine.'

'I don't know, bro. This girl. Sometimes I think she is rhubarb and I'm parsnip.'

Jack groans loudly, scrapes back his chair and returns to his books.

'Enjoy your porn,' Sanjay yells after him.

When they are alone, Sanjay turns his big stoned brown eyes on Joe. 'I think we could do it, you and me—the nursery. Your grey matter with my green thumb.'

'Sanjay, right now I feel like my grey matter is on a bench in a lab with first-year med students brandishing scalpels. They're laughing and the room smells of formaldehyde.'

Sanjay smiles his biggest, most winning smile. 'Well. You'll let me know soon, yeah?'

'I will.'

Sanjay spoons up the rest of Jack's tepid beans.

'Sanjay?'

'Joey?'

'You are a good friend.'

'I love you too, Joey.'

Joe goes up onto the roof to call Deck. They have a short, gruff exchange. It is different from being together, when the words were less important than the quality of the silence and the arc of the ball through the air: now he has to decipher the bumpy surface of their banter as if he were reading Braille. What Deck says is that he is bored; Lakes is the arsehole of the earth; they're all bogans who smell of fish, including his dad; he has to get the fuck out of there. But what he sounds is cheerful, showing no sign of taking off. His dad has been liaising with the school to have work sent up until they come to a more permanent arrangement.

'Maybe he could live here,' Jack suggests when he has climbed up on the roof with his guitar. Joe has been filling him in. 'We could look after him. He could be our mascot. Girls would love it.'

'I don't even know if that's legal,' Joe says.

'We're not going to adopt him. His parents would have to agree.'

'Where would he sleep?'

'Duh. In the lean-to.'

'Yeah. Right.'

20

Wednesday evening he runs to work. There are new leaves on the plane trees and the twilight is warm and sparkly. Fitzroy is full of boys in tweed and Brylcreem; girls in their grandmothers' dresses, long legs and short boots. He sails by in sweat and black cotton.

Pushes through into the dark closed bar. Straight away, he hears Lena singing in the kitchen. Listens as he stretches out his legs, massages his calves. It's the same lullaby. He's going to know it word for indecipherable word. Only when she stops does he call, 'Bravo!'

'*Grazie.*'

He goes out back and showers, changes into jeans and

t-shirt, apron; pushes through the swinging door into the kitchen.

'How long were you out there?'

'Not long.' Leans back against the wall to look at her. Her hair is messed up, she's not wearing any makeup and her cheeks are pink from the stove. She is frowning in concentration, popping little broad beans from their limp grey skins so fast he can barely see her fingers move. Unobserved, his eyes trace over the golden skin of her forearms, lingering on the faint scars from her occupational burns, up to her muscled, slender biceps. He skims her breasts under the old red t-shirt and finishes on the line of her neck, bent over the work surface.

The looking feels good. He breathes out. 'What are you making?'

'Broad bean mash to serve with grissini and olives. Dip of the day, my friend.'

'Nice.'

'Nice? It's going to be fucking sensational.'

He smiles. 'Lena, it's dip of the day.'

She looks up at him and down again, smiling too. They are both grinning but it is not that funny. He wonders what she saw on his face.

'What?' he says eventually.

'For a second there, you reminded me of a little boy waiting to lick the bowl.' She is still smiling.

'I'm definitely not helping you now.'

He pushes through to the dark bar again, scanning the room to see what needs doing.

'New cleaners are shit,' he calls back over his shoulder.

'I know. Tell Boss, would you? I've already mentioned it, like, seven times.'

'He won't care. They're cheap like him.'

Joe gets a hard broom and sweeps the floor; then a wet cloth to wipe down the tables.

'New girl on the bar tonight,' Lena calls.

He walks back into the kitchen and gets the box of mixed lettuce out of the cool room to wash. 'Yeah?'

'Look at you. I thought you weren't helping. Were you always such a good boy?'

He ignores this.

'I didn't think so. Anyways, she's hot, the new girl. Like, seriously.'

'I can handle myself.'

'I'm sure you can.'

Seconds later, Boss pushes into the kitchen with an armful of toilet paper and toothpicks. The new girl is trailing behind.

He must have picked her up en route and is laughing, expansive, turning on his petrol-fuelled charm.

'Heartbreaker,' Lena mutters to Joe.

'I give it a week.'

At five past seven they open doors and ten minutes after that the first customers arrive. By nine it is busy and loud. The new girl is unflappable and fast; a little sniffy but he likes her. Punters eat and drink and grow obnoxious, oblivious to the precise choreography of the staff that does their bidding. Hours pass.

'We're still waiting on the pizzas, yeah? They've asked me three times,' he tells Lena.

'Tell them to go fuck themselves.' She takes the glass of wine he proffers and has a gulp. 'Or they could just wait another five minutes.'

End of the night, there is vomit to mop up outside the toilet; he leaves it for the cleaners. Boss is taking the new girl out for supper. The kitchen hand leaves on the hour, crying headache, and Joe stays to help Lena pack up. They divvy up the tips and stand at the bench to eat leftovers. He offers to walk her home.

'I'm not scared of the dark,' she says, looking sideways at him.

'It's on my way.'

She cruises slowly beside him on her skateboard, one foot lazily hitting the pavement, and complains about the sparkie. He wants her to watch him play basketball every Monday night and gets sad if she doesn't.

'And do you cut the crusts off his sandwich too?'

'Get outta here, I don't even love him.'

Joe swallows his satisfaction. Tells her about the nursery and Todd—how he has been like a father to him. She listens and asks him what he wants. He tells her that's not the point. She tells him it is.

Until he has delivered her safely home. And they are standing outside her apartment talking in the dark. And then, without him quite noticing the progression, they are sitting side by side on the brick fence, smoking, while she tells him one of her curvy tales from the old world. He could listen to this shit all night. She asks if he wants to come in. He says no. So she reaches up and kisses his cheek and he lets his hand brush lightly down her golden arm.

Watches her go in, the door close, lights going on.

Runs all the way home.

You there, Joe?

Yeah.

I remembered something.

?

I thought you might like it.

The suspense . . .

She'd made an appointment at the hairdresser. She was going to get all her hair cut off really short, like Twiggy. Do you know I only just remembered tonight?

I don't know who Twiggy is or why you thought I would like to hear that.

She wanted to surprise you. You, Joe—she loved you.

He sighs. He is lying on his bed with the iPad. It's late. He wants to keep the sorrow at bay, so what is he doing back here?

She surprised me going out the window and getting smashed on the ground. That was a huge surprise.

Don't say that. Please.

We went to the Eureka sky tower on her mum's birthday. It has these angled windows so you can lean out. She said it was a well-known fact that people only get vertigo if they're drawn to jump. She liked being up high. She never got vertigo. I did.

She didn't jump, Joe, no one believes that. She'd been drinking and she lost her bearings.

I want to know what happened.

No answer; nor will there ever be.

If I'd stayed at the party she wouldn't have been alone in some stranger's bedroom sitting on the fucking window ledge.

*Yeah and if that boy hadn't had the party and if her friend
didn't give her that last cigarette and if she hadn't had so much
to drink or if she'd just stayed home that night or her brother
had gone to pick her up earlier like he said he would and if she
wasn't always doing such stupid things and if her parents were
not so self-absorbed . . .*

Are you done?

Are you?

Yeah.

I just wanted to tell you about the hair.

And sometimes the tigers just look sweet, like great soft
playthings—first prize on the shooting game at the carnival,
would you believe your luck? Take one home to the missus
to show you care. Hutan on his tummy by the water's edge,
huge paws furled and floppy; a rosy felt grin of a nose; fat pink
tongue lapping lazily at the pelt on his forearms. *I'll take five.*

You might imagine at these times, when the sight of the
cuddly cats has made you go soft, that it would be safe to
approach. Elise conjures a trapdoor into the enclosure, a metre
by a metre; imagines crawling through it on hands and knees.
Taking a moment, inside, to straighten up, brush off the dirt,

then strolling over with an offering of a brace of hens or a hindquarter of lamb. Leaning down to give Hutan a tickle under his fuzzy white chin and behind those hairy white ears that look, from behind, like the luminous eyes of a ghost; burying both hands into the thick scarf of fur around his neck.

She lives it through behind her dark glasses, sipping her coffee, smiling. How the tiger would chuff at her and roll onto his back to be stroked. She'd rest her face on that hot furry tummy; wrap the big cat up in her arms.

And then she'd be lunch.

No easel today, just her notebook and phone. She rereads the morning's text from Adam, after another late-night phone call that lasted almost two hours: *You say you don't know if you could trust me again. Maybe you don't need to know. Let me be the one to know this time. Let me carry you for a bit. A.*

She puts Adam back in the bag; returns to the cats. Aceh is on sentry, patrolling their territory. She thinks it is Aceh. Occasionally he veers off course, right to the back of the enclosure, has a sniff, then back to pacing the main borderline. Rainbow lorikeets have arrived with the milder weather and are making a racket in the treetops. The tigers pointedly ignore the birds, saving themselves for the odd possum or duck they take down each week, so that they may remember what they are.

They say tigers have exceptional memories, recalling significantly more, and for longer, than humans can. Perhaps these caged cats collectively remember being free: climbing trees, swimming rivers, tendering death. And perhaps a trip to see their wild cousins in India is not such a crazy idea. She has a credit card. If only she could pack Indrah in her suitcase.

The last holiday she had was before the start of Jennifer's final year. She took both her children to Laos; Adam stayed behind, on a case. They travelled the country on buses and trains; visited pagodas, wandered through rice paddies, learned to cook *mok pa*. The country was green and steamy and enchanting. Jennifer kept a journal and finished each entry with the daily bloopers. Elise will have to look for the journal—it should be in one of the boxes. She remembers thinking it was good to get Jennifer away from that relationship for a while, hoping some time out might lessen its intensity. It didn't.

She finishes the coffee and gets out the notebook, sits for another twenty minutes doodling. As she sketches the body of a young woman she can feel the cadence of her own heartbeat, her blood, muscle and bone. At one point she leans down and lifts the leg of her pants, turning her leg this way and that, picturing the orange and black stripes her daughter planned to have tattooed onto her calf. They would have looked incredible.

Todd's flat is sold via auction to a couple of newlyweds. Over a few days Joe helps his uncle pack up, accepting a trench coat that belonged to his grandfather and a set of brown fifties coffee cups. He draws the line at Todd's spare woollen dressing gown and dodgy collection of cookbooks. There are only so many ways to love tofu.

Late on the Thursday, Jack and Sanjay come to help load the trailer. A charity truck will collect Todd's remaining furniture, household appliances and crockery. The nursery is his stuff, Todd explains, seeming to forget he is trying to give that away too.

'It's a bit like shedding, yeah?' Sanjay comments as Jack is fastening the last octopus strap. 'You'd be a tree snake, Uncle.'

'You're right, Sanjay, this is going to give me a whole new lease of life.' Said like an affirmation stuck above a smeary mirror.

Joe looks back at the deadpan concrete building. 'You've lived here as long as I can remember.'

Todd scuffs Joe's hair. 'You were a funny little tacker. Oh, you made me laugh.'

'You were pretty funny yourself.'

Todd nods. They all nod, and nod.

Joe starts up his uncle's car, trailer affixed, and they drive in convoy to the house of the Wayward Wind. His mother fusses as they carry Todd's life up the path and into Joe's old room.

The room has been repainted but he can see small gashes in the plaster left by his old posters and photos. At least Todd brought his own bed. Joe's went out in the last hard rubbish collection and someone had carried it away by morning, innocent of all its packed-down memories.

'Uncle, you need plants in here,' Sanjay says. 'We'll smoke out the room too. We can have a ceremony. I feel the ghost of the delinquent Joe.'

'Getting stoned will keep the ghost of delinquent Joe here, idiot,' Joe says.

'No, no smoking,' Todd cautions, nodding towards the window. Joe's mum is out front with Jack, who feels obliged to sweet-talk all mothers.

Joe laughs at his uncle. 'What, you're not going to get stoned in front of her? How will that work?'

'I haven't worked it out yet. Any tips from the old days, Joe?'

'Yeah, go up onto the roof, you'll find an old collection of butts in the guttering, then lock the bedroom door and listen to the White Stripes really loud with your headphones on.'

Todd chuckles before sinking down onto the armchair plonked in the middle of the room, dropping his head into his mangled hands. 'Right you are, boys,' he mutters. 'Just a little tired now.'

Joe would like to yank Todd to his feet—like his uncle once did for him—and provoke him into fighting back against the shrinking of his world.

But it wouldn't help. So they collect Jack from his schmoozing and Joe leaves home once again.

21

'Remember that old road movie Sanjay made us watch? You are definitely Thelma,' Jack says, watching Joe pack his bag. Planning and preparation has been minimal but Joe is at least crudely folding clothes into Todd's old mustard canvas cast-off, while Jack's are balled into a green cloth bag lined with potato dirt.

'Yeah, so I score with Brad Pitt. Stick that in your pipe, Louise.'

Joe has taken off shifts at the bar and cafe to go on a road trip with Jack to Lakes Entrance. Jack needs a study break. Joe needs to see Deck. The plan is to find a cheap motel with flashing neon lights. They are taking a change of clothes, Jack's guitar, a bottle of Jack's dad's whisky—stolen, but Jack says he is owed—and cash. They are hoping to borrow fishing gear from Deck's father, or rent it, or buy a line and hooks from a hardware store.

At dusk on Sunday, Joe turns over the engine in the Citroen, lets it warm. He can hear the slow clank-clank of the driers turning in the laundromat and sees, through the window, a young couple on the nod on the orange plastic seats; slumped against one another, still connected as they dream their private dreams. He looks towards the back of the house, but there are no signs of life in the lean-to.

He sees the nurse less and less. A few days ago, he crept in there in the middle of the day. Touched her face and she flinched and rolled over, eyes masked. Soon she will be gone. Every time he takes leave of her is a dress rehearsal.

Sanjay has come out onto the pavement in bare feet to see them off. Wearing a turquoise kurta, his shiny black hair loose down his back. He gives them a joint as a parting gift. 'Look after my wheels or I will rip you to pieces with my bare hands.' He has an assignment due in three days that he hasn't started, but Emma is back so the world is his vegie bed.

They toot as they turn the corner, and then drive on out of town, watching the sun set over the Eastern Freeway with its occasional roadside sculpture that seems to ooze self-doubt:

Do you like me? Really? Am I okay? Jack has just handed in an essay on the changing legal landscape of aiding and abetting, and now he wants to pretend he is Kerouac. 'Just call me Jack,' he keeps saying, and laughing uproariously.

They drive for two and a half hours, channel flicking until they settle on a local station that sounds about twenty years out of date, so that it feels like they are moving through time as well as space. Until they hit Sale, where they eat under the bright lights of McDonald's, going back for seconds of the sweet airy buns. Even drinking the coffee.

Jack takes over the wheel then and after another hour, as they near their destination, lights up the joint.

'When the nice policeman asks I'm going to say it's yours and you made me,' Joe says. But he takes it and has some because he is starting to think you can be too careful.

'The Entrance!' Jack shouts through his wound-down window as they finally enter the outskirts of Lakes.

Velvet Underground comes on the radio. Joe turns it up. They pass a road sign that nudges, simply: WAKE UP TO YOURSELF. 'I'm definitely stoned,' he comments.

'I know, right? We are living the dream, right here, right now, in this moment.'

'That's a Top 40 song?'

'It should be!'

'It is.'

They laugh, but it is true that Joe wants to live this moment. In this moment, he doesn't wish he was dead. He winds down his window. It's cold but he can smell it: 'Can you smell it?' he asks Jack.

'What? The sweat of bogans?'

'No. The sea. Can you smell it?'

Jack takes a big cartoon sniff. 'Yes, I am getting sardines and saltwater in the foretaste and some rotting kelp at the back of my palate.'

'Let's go to the shore.' And with his mind bent, Joe is ten years old again on the back of his dad's motorbike, and any minute now they will arrive.

'Yeah, mate. Let's find a room, drop our stuff, head down.'

They hit the esplanade. The arm of water between the foreshore and the mainland is dark, flat, pungent; the glowing-red Floating Dragon restaurant is the lighthouse. Joe peers into darkened shop windows as they glide by, imagining how different all this would look by day. He can almost see the delivery vans pulling up, dogs following their leads, the putt-putt-putt of trade; which makes him think again of the nurse, who misses out on all that life. He should be glad for her she is leaving, if he loves her at all.

The first sordid-looking motel they come across is full—or did the woman just say that because she didn't like the look of them? At the next they get a twin room for eighty bucks. They pull the Citroen neatly into its allocated rectangle.

Jack slides the key into the lock and pushes the door open. 'Ah, perfect!'

They can hear at least three TVs on three different channels.

'It's just exactly as you would expect it to be,' Joe observes, throwing his backpack down on one of the beds, made up with a yellow-and-brown-chequered spread.

'Shower looks clean,' Jack calls from three metres away. 'Free breakfast is good.'

'Breakfast now would be good.'

They put on coats and beanies—the sea air is cold—and stuff whisky and tobacco in their pockets; lock the door behind them and walk to a servo to buy chocolate then head down to the inlet. Up close, the dark water becomes dynamic. They huddle side by side and watch its rippling mass, the uncountable noun. Jack passes Joe the whisky and he takes a swig. It warms him from the inside out. He's going to run with it.

'Are you looking forward to seeing your urchin?' Jack asks.

'Yeah. Yeah, I am.'

They eat the chocolate. The water laps gently at the shoreline.

'You're lucky, Joe.'

'I am?'

'Things come naturally to you.'

'Bullshit.' But guilt shoots through him like a strobe, a reminder from the mother ship. He *is* lucky—to be breathing this salty black air, blood pulsing through his veins. 'You're too hard on yourself,' he says to Jack after a while.

'Like you can talk.'

'I am.'

'I don't think I'm going to make it,' Jack suddenly confesses. 'With the law degree. I think I made a mistake.'

'Stop working so hard. Take your foot off the pedal.'

'I can't. I can't do any less. My dad's right. I'm only getting average marks as it is.'

'Your marks are fine; I've seen them,' Joe says.

'I don't think I can last the distance.'

'Kindly ask your dad to fuck off out of your head.'

'Yeah, well, that's easier said than done. First I don't do Law because he doesn't think I'm cut out for it—but is that why I'm doing it now? To prove something? I don't even know what I want.'

'You are not the first,' Joe says, taking the whisky again. 'You will not be the last.'

'Thank the elephant god for Sanjay, who is never hard on himself, who furnishes us with wheels and weed.'

269

'Thank you, Ganesh,' Joe agrees. 'Is that phosphorescence?'

'Where?'

'Out there, on the surface.' Joe points towards the little fishing jetty.

'You mean where the fisherman is pointing his torch onto the water? You fucking idiot.' They howl as if it is the funniest thing, that Joe mistook manmade light for something magic.

'Let's go see what they've caught.'

Up the jetty to the pergola. They start up a conversation with the two Italian fishermen: a father and adult son. They've got a nice set-up—couple of foldout chairs, esky with beers, bait and rig. They're fishing for calamari. Joe looks at them and thinks of his own dad, and how this is what might have been. Perhaps Jen is back at the motel now, warming the bed. He wraps his arms around himself: the air is bitter, and here he is, still—no father; no lover.

The men are up from Melbourne too, for a week of this. The son shows them the three squid in the bucket—*delizioso*. Joe and Jack accept a beer and sit on the bench seat, passing the whisky around, smoking and quietly talking themselves into woozy contentment.

When the father hooks another, Jack and Joe jump up and make a show of helping, holding the bucket at the ready, passing the long-nosed pliers. They cheer and hoot as the sucker is reeled in. It's a fat one, and beautiful, changing colour to a dark mottled purple in a vain attempt at camouflage. Giant head on little feet; huge vivid eyes that can see through light and dark; one of the most intelligent creatures in the sea, apparently; come to its final moments on a Sunday night in September surrounded by depraved men.

'Poor little bastard,' Jack says.

The father kills it quickly, mercifully, with a knife through its brain, and yanks it off the hook, dropping it into the bucket with the others. And for now, at least, small hearts stay inside small bodies.

'It's a good life, eh?' the older man says, reaching for Jack's whisky.

It's after midnight. The fishermen pack up, satisfied with their catch. They offer Joe and Jack one of the squid but there is no place to put it so the boys accept a last beer and they all promise to meet again on the jetty, some other night. Father and son carry their gear back to their Toyota HiLux and drive away.

They sit a little longer on the bench under the pergola.

'Maybe I could reel them in and you could finish them off?' Jack suggests.

'Lost your killer instinct?'

'Mate, did I ever have one? Lately I wonder.'

Joe remembers stabbing carp on the bank of the Merri Creek in the bright sunshine. He can see Jen's screwed-up face, hear her high-pitched squeal. He was trying to impress her, and impress on her—that he could provide and protect. It was the one thing his dad had given him, the hook, the knife, so it mattered. She didn't turn away. She wasn't scared of the blood.

'This is good,' Jack says as they're walking back to the motel. 'We have to do this more often.'

'Yeah. We should.'

'Tomorrow I'm going to sleep in. I'm not going to read any fucking decisions, and I'm going to eat fresh prawns.'

'Yeah, live it up a little, Louise.'

'Call me Jack.'

'Ha.'

They pull off their boots and jeans, and curl up in their single beds under their yellow-and-brown-chequered covers. They go out like lights.

———

She has arranged to meet Tom at a bar in the city, one of those dark, unadorned places evoking Prohibition, where the tenders are lush dames with tight dresses and big red mouths. After much adolescent deliberation, she has worn a black pencil

272

skirt and a green boat-necked jumper, new boots; mascara, no lipstick. The picnic in the hills was fun and flirtatious, a first date with someone you've known forever. This, a second meeting in a bar at night, is an escalation. She does some surreptitious deep breathing, orders a glass of wine and picks paint out of her fingernails.

And then he is thirty minutes late, gratuitously sorry. Straight from the office, he says he has spent nine straight hours in a waffle iron—how he hates a foregone conclusion. So they talk about his work, and the relentless pressures of finding funding. And she talks about a minor copyright issue on her latest job, which seems to fascinate him. Shows him a photo of the half-made quilt she has commissioned from Maddy, and complains that Carl is moving to Geelong to be halfway between work and the surf. She will see even less of him.

Tom reveals that his son is in serious debt and clinically depressed. How can he help without taking over? They're always accusing him of taking over.

'Well, it's better than doing nothing,' she points out. 'At least you are there for him.'

'Is it better? Perhaps I've prevented him from building his own capacities.'

Elise winces. 'Jesus, this is what we do in midlife, isn't it? Sit around wondering how badly we screwed up.'

'You do this too?' He smiles.

'You wish you'd been a better parent or a better role model, or even just enjoyed the time more, you know? The time you actually had together.' And then, to her shame, and without warning, a sob erupts from her private subterranean cave. 'Oh shit, I'm sorry.'

'You don't need to be.' He reaches for her hand. His skin is dry and warm.

'That just still happens sometimes. I'm okay.'

He threads his fingers through hers. Looks at her intently. 'It's fine, Elise. I understand.'

She looks back at him, aware of his thumb stroking across her fingers. 'Thank you,' she says, trying to match his sincerity, to return to the present.

'I've always fancied you, Elise. You know that. Don't you?'

So it has come to this—he is offering himself to her—but not in the way she'd hoped. The feel of his hand is wrong; the too-cool setting. And the conversation has conjured Adam: the father of her children. They should have stayed on neutral ground, but there is none. And just like that she knows. This was a sweet dream but there will be no deliverance here.

She smiles and squeezes his hand tightly before gently untwining her fingers from his, pretending she hasn't seen the strength of his need. 'Tom, you've made my week. I had such a big crush on you at uni. Ask Jill.'

He sits right back in his chair. But has to check. 'And now?'

'God, I wish life were simpler.'

'Could it be? Simpler?'

'I don't know, Tom. I'm so sorry if I misled you. I haven't done this in such a long time. But it's still so fresh, the separation.'

'*I'm* sorry—for putting you on the spot. I never was very patient.'

'If the timing was different . . . I used to hope you'd ask me out but you never looked my way.'

He manages a smile that doesn't quite reach his eyes. 'My loss.'

They stay for one more glass of wine, to save face, then go outside to hail cabs. A quick hard embrace. It's probably her loss, actually, but at least one she has chosen.

And it is so unexpected, how glad she is to arrive home alone; walking up the path, the amber lamp coming on in an automatic welcome. Unlocking their heavy wooden front door; up the corridor, flicking on lights, filling the kettle; her current painting bold on the easel in the middle of the kitchen. So glad to have avoided further complication that without much thought she sends Adam a text: *What do they say about the wisdom of no escape? I'll come along to meet this relationships wunderkind. No promises. Just to talk. Okay, sunshine?*

He texts back within minutes: *Very okay. Want to talk now?*

They lie in their respective beds and spill words into the dark, while tigers curl up in their corners, lulled to sleep. Every now and then Adam clears his throat and he could be right there beside her. They are recollecting, mostly. He remembers teaching Jennifer to ride a bicycle on the footpath outside the house, her huge gappy grin when she finally got it. She wore that ridiculous face for a week. He remembers how she would cling to his ears when he carried her on his shoulders and, much later, the torture of teaching her how to footnote an essay. She got so frustrated she threw a bowl of cereal at the wall.

'You remind me of her,' Adam says down the line.

'Yeah. You remind me of her too.'

———

Joe, you there?

—

I want to come clean.

—

Joe?

At exactly nine, breakfast is delivered to their room. Joe wakes to the sharp little knock; pulls on jeans and drags himself to the door. Jack is snoring loudly, as per. He takes the tray from the middle-aged woman in the flowery apron who looks him up and down as if he only need ask; thanks her, closes the door with his foot; prods Jack awake on the way to the bathroom.

They don't address one another until they have ripped open little cardboard boxes of Sultana Bran and started to eat. 'Delicious and nutritious,' mutters Jack. 'Feeling good, Joe, from the inside out.'

Joe grunts. Hangovers are shit.

Under metal covers they find rubbery eggs, cold toast, semi-cooked bacon curls, half a grilled tomato each sprinkled with dried parsley.

'Yum,' Joe says.

They eat it all and drink the tepid tea from the stainless-steel pots with the hinged lids.

'I feel like I need a drip in my arm to go with this,' Jack comments, 'and gaping blue pyjamas with my cock hanging out.'

Joe could tell him about the nurse—right now. Doesn't. 'You coming to see Deck?'

'Yeah, I want to see the little shit. His dad's taking us fishing, right?'

They shower, dress, leave the tray outside the room and get into the car, punch Pete's address into Google Maps. Joe drums a beat on the steering wheel as he drives; in part, there's the old fear he will fail Deck—but mostly he is excited.

They pull up in a quiet circle of houses and find number eleven. Deck is splayed across the couch on the veranda, playing on his phone. He flicks back his hair with a coltish toss and grins as Joe and Jack walk up the driveway.

'You've been waiting for us,' Joe teases.

'As if.'

Deck pulls himself to standing in one fluid motion. He looks taller. Maybe it's the way he's holding himself. He's got a bit of acne but he looks handsome in a floppy boy-band kind of way.

Joe pulls him into a headlock and messes with his pride and joy until Deck pulls free, scowling.

'Looking good,' Joe says.

'You're not.'

'Good to see you, man,' Jack adds.

'Where's your dad?' Joe asks.

'Shops. He thought he should get something special for your visit. I told him not to bother but . . .'

'You going to show us around?'

They go on a tour of the two-bedroom unit. The day

is mild and the windows all open. It is bare inside, almost monastic, and matt-clean. Deck's room is white over a bristly sage carpet. A single white bed and matching gold-trimmed bedside table bearing an empty glass and a stack of ancient *Mad* mags. They walk through the kitchen, the living room, peer out the back door at the patch of lawn that mirrors the front.

'You been doing much fishing?' Jack asks when they come back out to the veranda.

Deck groans. 'It's all I fucking do.' Relents. 'It's okay.'

'Keeping up with your school work?' Joe asks.

'Yeah. Are we done with the interrogation yet?' He reaches for Joe's tobacco.

Joe holds it out of reach. 'This will kill you.'

'It'll kill you too.'

'If I stop, will you?'

'No.' Deck leans over and snatches it.

'You spoken to your mum?'

'She rings every day. It's annoying.'

Joe nods slowly.

'She wants me to go back.'

'You probably want to stay here, right, with the golden sand and the beach babes?' Jack says.

Deck shakes his head. 'It's been good and that, but the school's full of clowns. I want to see my friends. And my girl.'

'Your *girl*?' Joe grins. 'You back together?'

'We've been talking.'

'There could be a room at our place, if you wanted to stay for a while,' Joe says.

Deck looks sideways at Joe.

'You can get Youth Allowance soon, right?' Jack says. 'Maybe your dad could help with the rent?'

Deck keeps looking at Joe, waiting for the punchline. 'Your place?' Laughs.

'I don't know—it could be an option, if you wanted to, if your parents were cool. You'd have to go to school, though, and behave like a human being. Or we would throw you out on your skinny arse.'

Deck smokes and looks at the ground, a slow smile opening his face—shaven, Joe thinks; maybe his dad bought him a razor.

'I can cook,' Deck says. 'Ask my dad.'

'Maybe you could teach this mama's boy then,' Joe says, tipping his head at Jack.

Jack rolls his eyes, says to Deck, 'Yeah, we can't be like your parents, you'd have to look after yourself, yeah?'

'What do you think I do?'

'Well, so think about it. Talk to your mum and dad.'

They move back to the fishing, Jack's new favourite topic,

and talk sinkers and line weight, hooks and bait, and let the idea of the room float on the salty air.

Deck's dad returns in his ute. Gets out with a plastic bag, kicks the door shut behind him. He is taller than Joe—Joe can only remember him sitting down at the kitchen table in front of Deck's birthday cake—and with the beard he looks like some sort of Lakes Entrance Viking.

Joe shakes his hand. 'Hi, Pete. Good to see you again. This is my friend, Jack.'

'Nice to meet you.' Jack puts out his hand.

And then they go inside and drink instant coffee and eat thick yeasty slices of Boston bun.

'Perfect hangover food,' Jack enthuses, cutting more.

'So you boys want to do some fishing?' Pete drawls. 'Nice north-easterly. Should be able to find you a few.'

'Cool,' Joe says.

'That'd be great!' Jack adds, sounding about twelve.

'Come on then.'

'It's like dad porn,' Jack mumbles to Joe as they follow Pete outside. 'Forget Deck, do you think he could adopt us?'

Joe laughs. 'Shut up.'

They hook the trailer that carries Pete's twelve-foot schooner onto the back of the ute and then Joe and Jack follow behind in Sanjay's pissy little car, turning local radio up high.

22

The Velvet Room at the base of the old theatre on High Street is packed with family, friends and a smattering of fans. Once a skating rink then a cinema for early talkies, through a dead era as a ballroom and lame reception centre, the theatre is now the favoured live-music venue for local acts. On the stage at the back of the room, band members are tuning instruments and the playlist; Sanjay is massaging Emma's shoulders. The audience mills, turning out the coarse flour of human intercourse: gushed introductions and half-meant kisses; unspoken questions, whispered promises; all the hope and hopelessness.

Joe and Lena are standing by the bar. The CD launch coincided with her night off so he asked her along. She is wearing a grey crepe dress circa 1940s—which didn't belong to her grandmother, because her grandmother wore rags and nearly starved to death. It clings to her body. He can't help but notice this.

'This is vile,' she says of the house red. 'If I wasn't a Cossack I couldn't drink this shit.'

He takes the glass from her hand and has some. It's shallow and sweet. 'It suits the room.'

'True.'

They look out together over the crowded space. Sanjay has moved offstage but is right up front, in his straight-legged jeans, pointy shoes and floral shirt. Joe also points out Vijay, just as animated and handsome as his son in clinging white cotton and immaculate coif.

And here is Lena, right next to him.

'So where's your squeeze?' she asks, reading his thoughts. 'Why isn't she here?'

'You're blunt as grandpa's fishing knife, Lena.'

'Well?'

'I don't know. Maybe she's at work? Maybe she's packing her bags.'

She ponders for a while. 'Do you want her because she is unattainable? Is that it?'

He shifts on his feet; doesn't want to do this with her. 'I always knew she was only passing through.'

He doesn't say that the nurse is fading like an old photograph; that what was vivid and vital is losing colour, and that sometimes it makes him unbearably sad.

'Exactly.' She's nodding. Smug.

'Interesting,' he gives back. 'How you seem to go for the attainable ones you don't want.'

She shrugs. 'I get lonely.'

Lights are dimmed. The room falls silent. A middle-aged hipster Joe doesn't recognise stands up to launch the CD, squeezing out piquant praise, and then the band starts.

Emma opens with a fiddle solo and the spirited command in her technique seems to demand a communal lightening. The other instruments join in and begin their inbred conversation, intricate and excitable.

Lena stands on her tiptoes, says into his ear, 'They're good! You didn't tell me.'

'I didn't know. I was trashed last time.'

She throws an arm up over his shoulder, all matey, and he smiles down at her, irritated and tender at once. And for a second he imagines leaning in to kiss her. He would like to communicate something with his mouth that can't be said.

He would like to slide a hand up under her grey crepe dress and make her wordless with excitement.

They watch the band, making occasional comments and observations to one another about the music, the people, but it gets so that all he can think about is her hand burning through his thin t-shirt. He is almost relieved when she lets it drop.

Towards the end of the second set, Jack arrives from a family dinner. He's been on the scotch—trying to keep up with his father—and his eyes are glazed and a little angry. Joe introduces him to Lena and then, through the final songs, notices Jack looking at her, shooting smarmy smiles. Scumbag.

The band finishes, lights widen, and there is more milling and a gradual sifting, till only the inner circle is left. Sanjay comes over, beaming, asking if they want to come on to another bar where the band has a private room. There'll be whisky and poker, more music. Jack needs more whisky and has to beat someone at something, but Joe makes his apologies. Has to be at the cafe early to open up.

'You should go,' he says to Lena, and then is glad when she declines.

Sanjay pulls Joe into an embrace as they're leaving, slapping his back. 'She's hot, Joey,' he says into his ear.

'She's a friend from work,' Joe says back.

'You go with that, bro.' Sanjay releases him.

He walks her home. It's a long way and they walk slowly. They talk about the music, and he asks her why she doesn't play an instrument. She explains that her dad played the trumpet when he was depressed, so to her it seemed like the instrument was making him sad. 'Singing seemed to make him happy.'

'Lena, your singing would make anyone happy.'

'Aww.' She puts her hand into his coat pocket and pulls out his tobacco. Helps herself. 'What would make you happy?'

Under cover of dark, he tells her about his dream of being a sports teacher.

'Uh-huh. Yeah, I can see that. You'd be a great teacher.' No big deal.

So he explains about soccer and hockey and basketball, and how they make implicit sense. How games have an inbuilt momentum and shape, and there are goals and penalties—rules for everything. When something is unclear you just listen to the ref.

'So there is no confusion?'

'Of course there's confusion. That's part of the game. But you know where you're going and what you have to do to get there.' And suddenly it sounds like an apology—or a plea. He can still feel the imprint of her hand.

'Do you wish there were more rules off-court, Joe?'

'Do you have to analyse everything, Lena? There is an infinite number of rules off-court. Ask your grandparents.'

'Yeah, but they broke the rules. They hated the rules.'

'There had to be rules to break. Or we couldn't function. Obviously.'

'Sometimes you remind me of a carthorse, you know? With those big blinkers on so you can't see what you're missing. I think you're afraid of how good things could be. Like really fucking good.'

'I don't even know what you're talking about.'

'Yeah you do.' She stops right there on the street and looks at him with naked eyes as she lights her cigarette.

She is brave, he thinks, but what he says is, 'Nah, I don't,' because he is not. He meets her eyes, though, and he lets her see that he is not wearing blinkers. And under the streetlight he sees her smile. And he smiles back.

They keep walking. 'You're hard work, sometimes,' she says. 'You're like a second job.'

'Thanks. And you're a walk in the park.'

They pull up outside her apartment. 'Lucky I like you so much, son of a carp.'

'Everyone keeps telling me I'm lucky.'

'Thanks for asking me tonight. It was fun.'

'It was.' He lingers though. 'I was thinking, you promised to make me *holubsti*.'

'Ha! You even remember the name. Okay, let's have Sunday dinner when I get a night off. You can wear your best embroidered shirt.'

'Cool.' He starts walking backwards. 'So I'll see you at work.'

'Yeah.'

And this time he doesn't wait until she has gone safely in. She watches him walk away, and he keeps looking back until he reaches the corner.

Runs home, light, breathless, detouring to the playground, where he pauses for a single dead hang in the dark. He makes it last seven minutes. He is almost there.

———

The night it happened. The call.

He was deep asleep and then the phone was ringing—the landline. A benign but incongruous sound, an irritant, he didn't think to worry as he heard his mother padding down the hallway and picking up. They had had their share of prank calls. *Hello?* he heard her say. *Who is this?*

Then, *Oh no*, too quiet and serious. The glowing green numerals on his bedside alarm clock said it was 3.17. But in that moment he was still innocent. Probably his estranged grandfather had died at last; this was his first coherent thought. And: why didn't they just call her in the morning?

He got out of the bed and went to her, his mother, in her distress.

She was leaning against the wall in the kitchen but he could see her by the moon, and the streetlight, coming in through the window. She was holding the phone to her ear. And she looked at Joe when she said, *We're coming*.

She put down the phone. She told him.

They were turning on lights, all the lights in the house, and they were dressing fast, urgent, as if they could still get there in time to pull her back in. Joe was swearing, *fuck, fuck, fuck*, pulling on jeans, shoes with no socks. Out the door into the dark and quiet suburban street.

His mother driving and trying to soothe him with meaningless words, but Joe could only swear, in mindless repetition, and sometimes he would say, *No*, and shake his head. Then he would swear again and then, *No!* so loudly his mother fell silent.

At the hospital it was easy to find a park. It wasn't visiting hours: it was dying hours.

His mother trying to embrace him in the lift and him pushing her back, dry-eyed, shaking his head and his eyes open so wide everything was in panorama. *No*, he said to her. He refused.

He refused.

Admitted through two sets of doors into the intensive care unit and a nurse in navy blue scrubs taking them to her curtained bed. Like a joke. Surprise! Like the photo booth where they kissed.

The nurse drawing the curtain back and Jen's parents and brother gathered around. She didn't look too bad, so an instant of blinding relief. Bandage around her head. Body all neatly tucked under a white sheet. Pale. Plenty of tubes. Sleepy face. Beautiful.

But Jen's mother sobbing in the brother's arms, moaning, *My baby.* Jen's father on the other side of the bed, upright and stony. Reassuringly calm. And then holding his hand out to Joe and clearing his throat to say, *I'm glad you're here. She's going soon.* And Jen's father's voice breaking—so that Joe broke too, started to cry like a baby, because it was true. They were the men who loved her. And they had failed.

The smell of disinfectant and chemicals and something desperately human and still alive: sweat, urine, blood. She was hooked up to machines that were disco-flashing coloured lights and numbers but the line of her heartbeat—like in the movies—was slow, so slow. Like an old man jogging. Like the tide at turning.

Why aren't they doing something? Joe asked, his voice loud. Because it was just the five of them standing around the bed, and Jen not opening her eyes to laugh, or cry, or hold out her arms to him for comfort. *Where are the doctors?*

They can't do anything, Joe, her father said. *They can't do anything.*

And the lights flashing and the numbers changing, and he kissed her face and let his tears fall all over her, the love of his life. *I'm sorry,* he kept saying, *Jen, I'm so sorry.*

There was a clock on one of the machines so that something as simple as time could be measured. So he knew it was exactly forty-seven minutes after the call that her line went dead.

———

Elise and Jill meet on the beach opposite Jill's apartment on Saturday morning for their annual spring swim. A couple of middle-aged wannabes in togs with extra breast support, splashing, diving to the bottom for shells, coming up to float for long peaceful moments on their backs—buoyant, as women are—looking up at a blue sky decorated with small white clouds.

The sky reminds Elise of an ad she did for a funeral parlour. It was so shit she couldn't look at it when it appeared in her local paper. It was six months after Jennifer's death and looking back she can see she unconsciously parodied the brief. There was rage in the sugar coating, the becalming bullshit, but the client was delighted by the blue expanse with the whimsical white font that flew across it like cirrus clouds. She took their money and repeat work. She wasn't a total idiot.

Everyone she knew was circling Jennifer's death as if by not talking about it, it might go away, tail between its legs. At first there were flowers and casseroles of kindness, but few of her friends could look her in the eye in the months that followed. She carried the shame of surviving her child. Jill was her lifeboat then, though she was grieving too. They were allowed to say what was on their minds—nothing was sacred except their loyalty to Jennifer and one another. Knowing she could talk each day to Jill kept her from going right under; that, and the need to still be a mother to Carl. Adam, he got a non-speaking part.

The water is mortuary-cold. They bob about in the shallows, determined, jittery and exhilarated, a couple of dozen chumps clustered together on a fifty-metre stretch of the shoreline, drawn out by the sun's lap dance. There is camaraderie among the strangers, as if they are the only brave people on earth.

One young man grins at Elise and she grins back and for a moment she is young again, with everything ahead of her. Not even a mother yet. Not even bereaved.

'Your lips are getting blue,' Jill observes. 'Let's get out.'

'And there was I, making eyes at the boy in the black trunks.'

'Yes, sweetie, he was definitely checking you out.'

They sashay up onto dry sand and wrap themselves in Jill's purple bath towels. Jill has brought down a thermos of coffee that she pours into tin mugs. Elise proffers the greasy white paper sack containing two almond croissants.

They shiver in their towels, eat their pastries, and talk about the new deputy at Jill's work.

'He's *nice*.' Jill looks surprised by this. Could just be her eyebrows.

'Nice how? Does he wear a hat and a holster?'

'Ha. No, he's just thoughtful instead of actively undermining. He asks how you are. He's brought back the Friday staff lunch. I don't know how long it will last—yesterday I could swear we were eating sandwiches with that anchovy paste I haven't had since I was a kid—but there is less griping already.'

'Mindy's nose out of joint?'

'Well, you know, always, so no difference there. She has no interest in what goes on outside her office. He's not making a power play I don't think. Or maybe he is . . .'

They walk back up to Jill's apartment. Jill showers but Elise gets dressed, wants to leave the salt on her skin; feeds Pip. He is stretched out on the couch looking at her with disdain, doesn't stir until she's put down his saucer of shrimp mornay. Elise scratches behind his ears, strokes down his soft, fat body. There is not much wild left in him.

'So Bandhavgarh National Park is the place we're most likely to see a tiger,' she says when Jill reappears. 'It's got the highest density and we'd want to go between April and June, when it's summer, so the tigers will be near the waterholes.'

'Aha. Timing sounds good. So you're taking this seriously?'

'I'm taking it very seriously. Look at my face.'

'Hey, let's go to a travel agency. Today. Just for fun. We'll get a real live person to sell us a dream.'

They catch the light rail into town, reading newspapers on their iPads, and then spend a couple of hours wandering in and out of boutiques, listening to a young busker, sharing a pot of tea and more cakes, and finishing up at a travel agency on Russell Street.

The girl behind the desk is about Jennifer's age—the age Jennifer would be—and she has a nose ring and gluey mascara. 'India, right?' She yawns conspicuously. 'And when will you be wanting to travel?' They walk out with a quote and a fistful of brochures.

'Bit of a lacklustre performance,' Jill complains when they get outside. 'We may as well have done it online.'

'Yeah, I think that's what people do. Doesn't matter. We got what we needed.'

'So are you in?'

They stand in the late afternoon on weary old Russell Street, with its mobile-phone shops and the heady bouquet of deep-fried samosa and sweaty delinquency. They have seen better days, like the street, but the salt is making Elise's skin tingle. 'Yes?' she says.

'Yes?'

'Yes, by Jove.'

'Woohoo!'

They part on the corner, full of plans, and Elise heads back to the empty house, silently shushing the tinny little voice that reminds her once again, just for the record, in case she missed it, that her beloved daughter is dead.

23

The nurse wakes him from a deep sleep; she is in her scrubs, whispering, 'It's beautiful out there. Come on.' Cool hand on the back of his neck.

Gets up, pulls on a tracksuit, lacing up his Feiyue. Silent.

They exit the house in the charcoal pre-dawn. The laundromat is lit up but vacant. Heading to the bridge via the playground, the laneway, across the rooftops. He falls behind so he can watch her. Jumps that would have been impossible a few months ago she makes without pause. She moves like honey off a spoon. Doesn't hesitate. She is full of grace and she will not fall.

At the bridge they warm up some more, balancing on the embedded tracks, running up the walls, a little *quadrupedie*.

Along the bike path, in the middle distance, a woman is carrying a blanketed parcel. They can just hear the faint newborn mewling. Must be the baby won't sleep. They watch the woman disappear behind the canopy of a tree, in the direction of the old wooden footbridge, Joe's first *lieu de memoire*. He hears the nurse sigh. 'Can we get out of here? Find somewhere new? It feels sad to be here today.'

And so they head south-east, and soon they are in a place they have never been before. Quiet backstreets. A Jeep with no wheels, up on bricks, in someone's driveway, eaten by rust. Inconceivably, a goat tethered to a fence. It could be another city, another world, and he keeps checking his peripheral vision, to see that she is still there. Reaching out at one point to take hold of her hand—though it's awkward to keep pace. Dropping it again so they can underbar a railing.

If they could just keep running.

'I don't want to go, Joe—I knew I wouldn't,' she pants. And then with resolve, 'But the timing is good.'

'It is?' They cross a green public space the size of a house block and clear the wooden bench in unison, like they meant it that way.

'You've got a lot on. Deck. The girl at the bar really likes you—and I'm not even jealous. Okay, I am. But you've got the rest of your life. You don't need this.'

He looks: she is still there. 'How is the timing for you?'

'My timing has always been shit, but then you know that.'

Why does he let this go through?

They circle back, finding their way to the playground near the house just before dawn. Swing up into the cubby that forms part of the fort, contorting through its little arched entrance. He almost has to fold in two but they make it work, with the nurse between his legs, her back pushed up against his front.

The internal walls of the cubby are covered in graffiti: adolescents loving and shitting on one another, all the fucked-up passion and rage of youth.

'Remember how it felt?' she says.

He is slow to answer. They don't talk like this, but maybe the rules have changed now she is leaving.

Finally, 'Yeah, I remember. I was full of shit. I was careless. And when it really mattered I wasn't where I should have been.'

'We were *all* careless, Joe. Me especially. We thought we were so clever and funny. But we loved each other and we were loyal like hounds.'

'If I could play it again I would play it differently.'

'Don't say that. *Please*. No regrets.'

'Who would I be without my regrets?' Slides his hands down her thin arms until he is covering her hands with his.

'Sometimes I imagine you are coming with me,' she says quietly. 'I have this fantasy of us flying off together into the sunset.'

'And you're saying this *now*?'

'It's a fantasy.'

He buries his face in her black hair. And doesn't argue. Because he knows it will not happen—they're not going to rendezvous in some exotic foreign city to run, climb and jump, do impossible things, because she is peeling away. Because he is half in love with a girl with scars on her arms and a voice like an angel. And yet, and still, everything about the nurse feels right; smells right; tastes: light, like the air, like trees and water. Like first love. 'It's a nice fantasy,' he murmurs. 'You and me and the sunset.'

She twists around to look at him. 'When you're out like this, playing in the city, will you think of me?'

'On every cat leap.'

Anxiously, a little threatening even, 'Don't forget.'

'I couldn't—even if I wanted to.'

———

Elise touches the hard crusty face of the tiger with her finger-tips. The paint is almost dry. On this most recent canvas, the cat in the tree has coalesced with its prey. The limp human form is hanging now from a branch, bent in the middle like an acrobat. And from between its splayed legs Indrah's intense gaze burns out. Fur softening into skin. What is this thing? Is this thing dead or is it alive?

She doesn't know, but the painting is done. She delivers it to the laundry bench to finish drying; closes the door after her. There is, of course, no one to hide this work from, though she is perhaps still keeping it from herself. Not ready yet to take it seriously. Not inclined to stop. She will keep going until she finds the ending.

Goes back to the kitchen table, shears off a new length of canvas from the roll, fills her mouth with tacks and starts stretching.

She can feel the tigers stalking her, at a distance, and she is entertaining a return to realism in a portrait of the Bronx man jumping. It must have taken exceptional power and grace to leap from the monorail into that cage. And did the man feel 'at one' with the tiger as he'd so desperately hoped? The reporter never said.

The thing in the painting is dead. The thing is alive. The tiger owns it.

When she's finished priming the canvas she leaves it on newspaper to dry. Gets into the shower. She is meeting Adam for dinner up the road. And she won't tell him this yet but she thinks she might want him to come home. Hell, she is a risk-taker. Just like her daughter.

He has changed these past months as he has come undone. So has she. For the first time since Jennifer's death they can see one another. And now when she thinks about the sadness at the heart of their marriage, all the wan little gestures— pyjamas warmed by the iron, the bread, the footy, the cursory kisses—she thinks they were indicative not of disease but of an enormous feat of survival.

And contained in his brain are all those memories Elise will never be privy to. All the times she wasn't there. Things Adam knows about their daughter; conversations and understandings they shared. Sometimes it was too much, the way they adored one another. Elise wanted him to give Carl the same unconditional love. But then when Adam was absorbed by a case, Jennifer would be the most hurt and Elise would resent him for that, too. He is the keeper of all this and in his heart carries the same grief and useless love.

So she dresses in jeans and a t-shirt and musses her hair. Feeds the sourdough starter. Takes a swallow of wine straight from the bottle. Smears on a coat of tawny lip gloss. Primed for, like, whatever.

The old man hasn't turned up for the second week in a row. Joe keeps looking for him, willing him to appear, obstructive walking frame and all. Maybe they're fixing the other eye. Otherwise the morning brings the usual twanging chord of young mothers, aspiring writers, students and retail workers. He makes coffee after coffee, plates up, washes dishes, flirts, tallies, sweeps, sluices, till he is light-headed. After the lunch rush he takes a break and sits out back to read the paper. Eats an apple, smokes a cigarette.

In the afternoon, while Georgie keeps shop, he helps Voula with the moussaka. Peels and chops a head of garlic, devastates a bunch of parsley with a mezzaluna whose wooden handles are smooth as skin; whisks a dozen eggs into a bowl of cream. Runs out of tasks, so perches on a stool to watch. Voula's methodical movements are slow and ingrained, they seem to reach back in some clean, lineal way, while Lena, with her different burden of history, is tart and bird-quick.

'So how is your friend, the runaway boy?'

Joe fills her in and Voula makes a face of horror over her white sauce. 'He's gonna stay at *your* house?'

'Yeah.'

'Darling, you're just a boy. How you gonna look after him?'

'Voula, you insult me.'

Deep throaty laugh. 'Sorry, you are a big man. Here, big man, start frying the eggplants.'

Joe does.

'Is he a hard worker, your boy?'

'When he needs to be. He's smart—smarter than me.'

'Okay. I'll send him to my brother. He can go there after school.' Voula never had children of her own because she couldn't find a husband. 'My brother needs help and he's stubborn.'

'Voula, he can't even drive. He's fifteen.'

'Doesn't mean he can't change tyres.'

'Ha. His little girlfriend would love that.'

'Then he has some money for the rent.'

'You're an angel, Voula.'

'Darling, my brother pays the minimum wage. And you're burning the eggplant. Move!'

Runs home along High Street, diverting into the laundromat to collect clothes and towels that have been sitting in one of the driers for two days. Bounds up the three steps to the front door. Finds the key in its nook.

Jack is working at the living-room table. The door to the lean-to is closed; it seems to emanate absence.

'Yo,' Joe calls, kicking off his runners, massaging the soles of his feet.

'Rhubarb crumble from my mum,' Jack calls back. 'Help yourself.'

Joe does. Has it cold, drowned in supermarket-brand cream. The cream might be slightly off so he eats fast.

Jack comes in, sits opposite him at the kitchen table. Takes another helping and finishes the cream.

Joe gestures to the fence outside the window. The colour is almost completely leached from the painted ivy. 'We should touch it up. I've grown attached to the sad love vine.'

'Wasn't her point that nothing lasts? I can't even remember her name.'

'Bullshit.'

Jack laughs. 'Okay, it was Gemma, with the lisp and the breasts.'

'She had breasts?'

'Yeah, and I could play with them whenever I wanted. Fuck I need a girlfriend.'

Their seven-legged spider friend has moved into the kitchen and is hanging out a couple of feet above the window, stalking the flies that have come with the warmer weather.

'Your mother does a nasty crumble.'

'Don't mention my mother when we're talking about breasts. What about your chef then, you been stripping onions with her?'

'I wash her limp lettuce.'

'You like her, though. You do, don't you? Come on.'

'She's a friend.'

'And?'

'She's cool.'

'Maybe you could put me forward.'

The idea is reprehensible. 'No way.'

'Fuck you too.' Jack picks up his guitar from where it is leaning against the wall and makes music. Effortlessly. *'If you don't want her you should give her to me,'* he croons.

'What is this, the Middle Ages?' The thing is he does want her. He is starting to want her badly.

They hear the key in the lock, Sanjay returning. And before he even ducks in to say hi, on comes the Bollywood. The woman's lovelorn call is harrowing enough before a male voice responds. It sounds like he is having his toenails pulled off.

'And right there is a case where having a girlfriend has not improved quality of life,' Jack notes.

24

In the end, it is not so hard to let his uncle and Sanjay down. Fuck knows he has done it before.

It's a glorious spring day—twenty-five degrees, the sky cerulean blue. The earth has extroverted, all scented and rosy-cheeked, so they are having smoko outside the kitchen-office amid the greenery. Two customers are quietly browsing.

Todd in his foldout chair, wearing navy blue tracksuit pants and a mushroom-coloured jumper with gaping holes at the elbows—moving in with his sister hasn't lifted his game.

'Your mother shared a joint with me last week,' Todd tells Joe. 'We sat on the back step and looked at the stars.'

'Don't tell me things like that.'

But Sanjay beams at them both before breaking into his Mumbai shtick. 'I am liking your family more and more *every* day. My mother would be first making love with the Chihuahua before partaking of the holy smoke.'

'You can't talk about your mother like that,' Joe says.

They drink their coffee and Joe doodles on the back of a receipt pad, drawing the bridge and his own stick figure, the dotted line of the jump. Until he senses he is being watched. He looks up.

Sanjay clears his throat and steeples his hands dramatically in front of his chest. 'So this time I have news. My father has agreed to lend me the money for the nursery, Uncle, if the offer still stands. He hopes his good-for-nothing son will finally do something that doesn't shame him.'

'The offer most certainly does,' says Todd, sitting up straighter in his canvas chair. 'You little ripper, Sanjay!'

Joe is standing with his back against a post. Puts down the pad and pen.

'What do you say, bro? Come with?' His friend woos with those snake-charmer eyes.

Joe drops slowly down into a squat, until he is level with them both. 'Did I tell you I was thinking of going back to study?'

'Oh, your mother said something about that,' Todd puts in. 'I wasn't supposed to mention it. Can't you do both?'

'You know the peat moss and the black spot and the bare-rooted whatever? It means nothing to me. I've searched deep within but, I'm sorry, I'm going to pass.'

Sanjay gives him the full face of his disappointment. You can almost hear the sitar starting up. 'I had dreams for you and me.'

'I tried to put myself there. I did. But I'm more concrete and caffeine, you know that.'

'Sanjay?' Todd asks anxiously.

'Uncle, I'm good for it. I had considered this eventuality. Indeed, I saw it coming.'

Joe kicks Sanjay's foot. 'I'll help. I swear.' Sanjay scowls. 'And Lena, from work, she's always wanted her own place, I was thinking maybe she could make you a little menu for the weekends. Something basic.'

And Todd, he doesn't seem bothered in the least. He is beaming. 'I'm so damned proud of you both.'

Joe laughs. 'Lucky you're so easy to impress.'

'Speak for yourself, dickhead. I know how impressive I am.' Sanjay is wounded, but he wears it well. 'Go and buy us a six-pack of cold lager to toast the future of this fine establishment. Go now before I kick you back.'

Later, at sundown, he runs to the bridge, passing a young couple on a bench sharing an ice-cream. They are passing it back and forth, sugared up and happy.

Because he had a beer he stays close to the ground, practising the cat leap onto the concrete platform. Ten out of ten. Fifteen out of fifteen. Twenty out of twenty. It is fluid and tight, the training finally kicking in. Until his lungs and the palms of his hands are burning.

Runs to work. Where Boss is in a temper and Lena is clanging pans and cursing, a demented scarf around her head, looking gorgeous.

He showers, changes and starts setting up. It is true: he is lucky.

———

Wild tigers could be extinct in just a few decades—a possibility so devastating she cannot hold it in her head. So she squats before the first glass window—Indrah is prone beneath the low wooden shelter—and sips the sweet black coffee in her keep-cup, breathes in the blossom, tiny kid gloves opening in a tease of apricot, giving off their damp, bruised musk.

Two schoolboys approach in grey wool shorts and black lace-ups, holding bedraggled activity sheets in front of them like white flags. They are lugging knapsacks so overloaded they could be stuffed with the severed limbs of dead chums.

'It could get out if it wanted to,' one mutters to the other. 'You'll see. Up further there's this bit where it could jump out.'

'Nah. That's bull.'

Indrah has stopped grooming, meanwhile, and does seem to be particularly taken by the second one, with the ginger hair—the disbeliever. Elise has never seen her look like this before. She is completely still—smitten; her eyes are enchanting. So *this* is the death stare: it is quite different from the intense but speculative looks Elise has shared with the cats. It is so damned hungry.

'Ooh, he wants to eat ya!' the first boy says.

Ooh is right, and the ginger boy does now appear delectably pink and fat. Elise swivels between the two of them, almost jealous.

Boy 2 sniggers, a little edgy, and then uses all his will to break eye contact, turning to take a few steps away from the glass.

But you never turn your back on a tiger—they say that.

In a sequence as smooth as it is blood-quick, Indrah pulls up through her hind haunches out of the shelter and charges noiselessly, shockingly, at the boy, landing with her forefeet up against the window at shoulder-height. A huge guttural roar, entirely brutal, trumpets his demise.

The boys have frozen. And only when they understand that the tiger has been stopped in her tracks by the wall of glass do they reanimate, running back to the main path. Arms around one another's shoulders, swearing like their big brothers might. Their high-pitched laughter rings out as they beat a knock-kneed retreat.

All is quiet again in the jungle. Elise notes that through this drama, though her heart is wildly thrumming, she has not moved an inch. Her body did not rise in fright or even in an instinct to protect. Was she egging the tiger on?

She walks right up to the window and breathes out a small oval of steam onto the glass. Indrah, back on all fours, looks briefly into Elise's eyes, and though it can be nothing of the sort, what Elise experiences is recognition.

'See you next week, beautiful,' she says out loud. Grabs her satchel and heads for the exit; adrenaline still pulsing through her veins as she unlocks her bike, puts on her safety helmet.

And the first boy, well, he may just have been right. Across from Elise's preferred bench seat, where the barrier is low, and the tiger stalks the far shore of a narrow band of murky green water. If the cats were not so well fed, so utterly captivated, perhaps they really could. Like that hundred-and-fifty-eight-kilo Siberian at the San Francisco Zoo that astounded zookeepers and mathematicians alike by jumping across a thirty-three-foot moat, over a twelve-and-a-half-foot wall, to freedom.

25

He manages to get his hands on a bottle of Nemiroff *horilka*—
Ukrainian vodka; has to run a long way to get it and it costs
half a day's pay. Then on the Sunday in question he showers and
walks, all nice and mellow now, to her apartment. Pauses outside
the door, forehead against wood, to listen to her crooning. He
could scale the bars of her voice with his bare hands.

Knocks.

She's wearing skinny black jeans and a turquoise t-shirt
under a butcher's apron stained by a thousand ingredients.
Her feet are bare and he thinks she might be wearing mascara.
He'll take that as a good sign.

Hands her the brown paper bag. 'Smells good in here, Lena.'

She takes out the shovel-shaped bottle and oohs. 'You can come again.'

He sits at her kitchen table and she gets out two small glasses. 'We're going to have this neat,' she explains, 'because it's too good to drink any other way.'

He doesn't really like vodka but needs must. He takes a drink. The little blue and red apartment is twinkling, last rays of the day's light finding their way in to bounce off the white walls. They could be in an Eastern European seaside village inside a snow globe, all transporting and exalting and kitsch at the same time.

She is swilling the *horilka* around her mouth, eyes closed, making little sighing sounds. He smiles at her unseeing face. It strikes him that she is shameless—in a good way.

Opens her eyes and she is back to business. 'Can you put on some music?'

'Where's Carver?' he asks, looking through the playlist on her phone.

'Up on the roof probably, chasing birds.'

'Sounds fun.'

And suddenly he is dithering about what music to choose. As if it matters. So he realises he is nervous. The power has shifted—when did that happen? How? He goes with T-Rex.

She brings the dish from the oven and uses a paperback book as a trivet. Clinks her glass against his. 'So here are the little doves.'

She watches him as he takes a mouthful. He nods, takes another, makes her wait for it, grins. 'It's good, Lena. It's really good.'

And it *is* good, this dish from Mother Ukraine; the second mouthful even better than the first. The flavours are simple and slight but pure, texture sublime—it is solace served neat like the vodka. He can picture plucky little Lena with her plate of little doves, grandmother hovering, having her world rocked. With each earthy mouthful he is pulled deeper into her story.

He helps himself to more. 'You can stop watching me now. See? I'm loving it.'

'Do you think I could serve this at the bar?'

'You could get Boss to bring in the *horilka* too. Serve them together. The hipsters would love it.'

'We could call it Death to Putin.'

It is growing dark outside and she lights a fat candle that has just a centimetre of life remaining. He puts his feet up on one of the chairs. She has taken off the apron and the transfer on her t-shirt advertises Sea World. 'So the *holubsti* turned you on to food. Tell me another moment that made you.'

She smiles. 'So now you like this game?'

He smiles back. 'It's okay.'

'Okay, let me think. Year 9. First kiss—I was a late bloomer. Rory Skinner in grey shorts smelling of mandarin and sweat. He was from the brother school. We would meet at the bus stop every afternoon. I liked him because he was so different from my father in every imaginable way. He made me laugh.'

'That's sweet. Lucky Rory.' He starts rolling a cigarette and then she puts her feet up onto the spare chair beside his, so they are touching just ever so slightly. 'You want me to roll you one?'

She nods, so he does; lights it before passing it to her.

'Okay, your turn,' she says. 'A moment that made you.'

'Okay.' He runs his hands over his face. 'Okay. A couple of years ago, I saw a clip on YouTube. Of someone doing parkour.'

'Isn't that people doing jumpy stuff on buildings?'

So he tries to explain it to her: *l'art du deplacement*. About the beauty and precision, the fear and the implausibility. About moving forwards and overcoming with grace. Never giving up—especially when it's hard. Coming to trust your body and your mind so that when the shit comes down you will be ready.

'So you make yourself into an animal then.'

'Ha. Yes. Sort of.'

'That's cool. Can I come and watch you some day?'

'It's not really a spectator sport.'

'Well, I'm not going to *do* it. I'd break my fucking neck.'

He stares at her and it's like someone has picked up the snow globe and shaken it—he grows still because he needs to limit the damage. Sitting across from Lena his brain is conjuring a beloved and broken body that appeared strangely intact on the hospital cot. Someone always gets hurt.

He gets out his phone, frowns at it. 'You know, I've got stuff tomorrow. I should probably go.'

'Joe, what just happened?' Her face is puzzled, head tilted to one side. 'You do this,' she says. 'You're here and then you're gone.'

'Isn't everyone?' She is asking too much.

She ponders; shrugs. 'Okay, sure. Yes. But Joe—I want you to stay a while.'

She smiles now, imploring him. The air in the room is loaded up and there is a little pressure between their feet. It is a foot flirtation.

He ripples his fingers, does a big mocking sigh. 'I don't know what it is with you, Lena. You don't want to play by the rules.'

'Neither do you. And anyway you keep changing them. And I don't want everyone's story, Joe. Only yours. So come on. Tell me another moment that made you.'

It's been such a long time since he spoke her name out loud. And in this cheap souvenir of an apartment, with the faint smell of cabbage, and vodka at the back of his throat, he is truly afraid. *And you thought I was fearless, Jen.* But when he gets to the bit about the carp and the first kiss, beside the footbridge under the weeping willow—the punch of first love—Lena is grinning back at him. And later, when he gets to other parts, she is shamelessly crying. In his peripheral vision the nurse is disappearing over rooftops, light as air, but right here there is Lena, warm and alive. He is pulling her into his story.

The candle burns out and the room is corner-lit by a standing lamp so that their faces are in shadow.

'Joe,' she says finally, wiping her eyes. 'I understand now why your heart is so broken. Life is so fucking indiscriminate. I wish that had never happened to you.'

He shrugs. 'It didn't happen to me.'

'Yeah, it did.'

They sit in silence for a long while watching one another's silhouettes. He feels looser now, like any move is possible.

She lifts the bottle—in a question—and he nods. She refills their tiny glasses. 'Don't worry, son of a carp. I'm not trying to get you smashed so I can take advantage of you.'

'You don't imagine I might take advantage of you?'

'I'm a big girl.'

He pushes harder against her foot. 'Lena, is that an invitation?'

'Jesus, Joe, I posted you one of those about six months ago.'

'I don't like to rush a response.'

But then he pulls his chair in, leans over and lifts her foot right onto his lap. The possibility of her has come slowly, is a thing to savour. Keeps looking at her face while he strokes her sole with his thumb, reaching up her leg a little way under the cuff of denim. She is looking right back.

'Your jeans are sort of in the way,' he says, half smiling. 'Maybe you could take them off.'

So she stands up, walks around the table. He pushes his chair right back so she can straddle him. Which is what she does. She is so beautiful. Sliding his hands up her forearms, over scars from hot ovens and sharp knives, her biceps, triceps, deltoids, clavicles, up her neck and into her hair. Pulling her warm mouth down onto his. Finally ready to take the advantage.

On the man roof, Wednesday night, the sky spangled and the scent of jasmine floating up from the side fence.

'I'm going to come and film you doing the jump,' Jack says.

'No you're not.'

'I am, I'm going to put it on YouTube. And then you'll get arrested and I'll have to defend you in court. Ha!'

'Ha.'

There were only two beers in the fridge so they are passing them around, trying to make them last.

'Emma is writing me a song.' Sanjay leans back, hands on his narrow chest in a show of manliness.

'I'm still struggling to understand what she sees in you,' Jack says.

'Where do I begin? Astounding physical form. Charisma. The advanced study of the Kama Sutra.'

'I think it's your parsnips.'

They can hear the revolution of the driers in the laundromat; it is the soundtrack to their lives.

'Hey, you two were right about the chef by the way,' Joe says. 'Turns out I do like her.'

'I knew it, bro!' Sanjay says. 'She's like the perfect Joey lady. You could see that from about ten miles off.'

Jack groans. 'Oh well, that's just fucking wonderful! You can both just fuck off now with your hot girlfriends. I don't want to hear about it.'

'Emma has this cute cousin. I could line it up.'

'Used to be I was the one doing the pulling round here . . . now even the urchin got hooked up.'

'Hey, Joey—on that: we gotta fix up the room for your little friend,' says Sanjay. 'The windows are jammed shut and the door doesn't close properly.'

Joe sits up slowly. 'Huh?'

'I'm saying maybe you need to get the room ready. The cobwebs and shit.'

'Yeah.' Ice shoots through his veins. 'Of course.'

'Shit, bro, you get concussed under that bridge or something?'

'No, there's just something I have to check.'

Climbs down the ladder. The door to the lean-to is wide open. Tries to switch on the light but the globe has blown so he fetches a new one from the laundry cupboard, where Vijay keeps them, and twists it on.

Lighting up the absence.

A bare cell of a room with its white walls, web dangling from the ceiling. And no farewell note, no rubber clog left so he can go looking for her in this vast kingdom. But the windows are not jammed shut: they are open, every one, and a cool watery breeze is falling in. His metal ruler is lying on the dusty ledge, and he knew she was only passing through. He knew he couldn't keep her.

You there?

Yep.

It's been a while.

You okay?

This is going to sound asinine.

It probably won't.

I saw her—really saw her. She was strong and she was beautiful. Older and calmer. She was going on a big trip, she never said where.

Joe, you're making me cry.

No, it was good.

It's just I see her too. I want to get close but I can't.

I got close. I got very close.

Lucky you.

You really loved her, huh? Whoever you are.

He is smoking in his room again. The window wedged open to let the night in and the pollution out. Sanjay will never know.

Yeah I loved her and you're playing me like a harp tonight, Joe. I'm a mess here. I've been wanting to thank you actually —but you haven't been in here lately. I want to do it F2F.

Shit. Now I get to see the five heads? I don't know Emily Dickinson . . . what would you want to thank me for?

So this is the thing. Can you meet me at the zoo next Thursday? There's something I want to show you.

26

He runs to the bridge at first light. Warms up. His heart is beating hard but he has flow: every bone and muscle and tendon and ligament working together. Turning him into an animal—sort of.

Pulls up onto the orange steel girder and sidles nicely into position. Doing it all by feel. He's right up high and it's beautiful. He's not looking down. A nest of squabs flutters and coos. Spitting into the palms of his hands to smear the saliva onto the bottom of his Feiyue then rubbing hands together until they are warm and damp so he won't slide off the dust.

He will not jump too quickly and he will not wait too long. Lifting his heels now against the vertical of the too-narrow ledge so that he is on the balls of his feet, calf muscles and quadriceps engaged: committing. And maybe no trick he pulls off is ever going to bring her back but this one—it's for her. He is going to make a perfect landing.

Breathes: One. Two. Three. Four. Five. Leaps.

ACKNOWLEDGEMENTS

The first draft of this novel was written in a cell at the Old Melbourne Gaol and the second at the back of a community hall; thanks to Writers Victoria, the National Trust and Northcote Uniting Church for providing these dreamy spaces, and to Christa Gockel and her cats for sharing their Saigon pad while I found the ending.

Zookeeper Nardine Groch kindly told me stories about the tigers, and Kylie Saxon, Nina Davine and Philip Harvey offered nursing riches. My gratitude to Katya Brandon and Olga Radywyl for Ukrainian tidbits both literal and figurative. And for demonstrating a few moves under the bridge and providing a parkour precis, a huge thanks to *traceur* Harley Durst. *All mistakes are mine.*

Rachel Jones, Kate Ryan, Fran Cusworth and Kate Jones were early readers and gave invaluable feedback. Thanks also to my long-time writing group—Maryrose Cuskelly, Sam Lawry, Spiri Tsintziras, Wendy Meddings and Jane Woollard—for the eyes and ears. And to Miriam Rosenbloom for building me a beautiful new website.

Many thanks to Jacinta Di Mase for her steadfast literary agency and to Jane Palfreyman for taking the leap with such warmth and enthusiasm. I am indebted to Christa Munns, Ali Lavau and Clare James for their exquisite editorial attention, and Christa Moffitt for the killer cover. Working with the people at Allen & Unwin has been a total joy. Thank you.

It would all be as naught of course without the love and kinship of family and friends, including those who left the party way too soon—you will never be forgotten. Most especial thanks to James, Marlon and Llewellyn for their generosity and good humour and the precious insights into the minds of boys and men.

Ten per cent of royalties from this book will go towards the WWF Save Tigers Now campaign: www.savetigersnow.org